# "Are you attracted to Brian?" Michael demanded

Lorelei wondered if Michael could possibly be jealous and was surprised to discover that she hoped he was. "Are you asking as a private detective?"

"No. I'm asking as a man who once asked you to marry him."

He wasn't touching her. Not really. His fingers were merely playing with the ends of her hair. But as his knuckles brushed against the bare flesh of her shoulders, Lorelei felt as if he'd touched a sparkler to her warming skin.

"I'm more attracted to the tall, dark and dangerous type," she whispered.

"Dangerous?" He arched a brow.

"Dangerous." She touched a hand to his cheek and felt the muscle tense beneath her fingertips. "Dangerous to my mind." Her fingers stroked the side of his chiseled face. "Dangerous to my heart." Down his neck. "And incredibly dangerous to my body." Her free hand took hold of his and lifted it to her left breast. "Feel what you do to me...."

The author of over fifty novels, **JoAnn Ross** wrote her first story—a romance about two star-crossed mallard ducks—when she was just seven years old. She sold her first romance novel in 1982 and now has over eight million copies of her books in print. Her novels have been published in twenty-seven countries, including Japan, Hungary, Czech Republic and Turkey. JoAnn married her high school sweetheart—twice—and makes her home near Phoenix, Arizona. Look for her latest single-title release, *No Regrets,* available from MIRA Books now.

## Books by JoAnn Ross

### HARLEQUIN TEMPTATION

Don't miss any of our special offers. Write to us at the following address for information on our newest releases.

Harlequin Reader Service
U.S.: 3010 Walden Ave., P.O. Box 1325, Buffalo, NY 14269
Canadian: P.O. Box 609, Fort Erie, Ont. L2A 5X3

# MICHAEL:
# THE DEFENDER
# JoANN ROSS

## *Harlequin Books*

TORONTO • NEW YORK • LONDON
AMSTERDAM • PARIS • SYDNEY • HAMBURG
STOCKHOLM • ATHENS • TOKYO • MILAN
MADRID • WARSAW • BUDAPEST • AUCKLAND

ISBN 0-373-25754-6

MICHAEL: THE DEFENDER

# 1

EVEN AFTER all these years, Lorelei Longstreet was, without exception, the most stunning woman Michael O'Malley had ever seen. The long silk slide of hair falling over her bare shoulders was the improbable hue of a palomino's tail, but Michael, who'd known Lorelei back when her remarkable white teeth were wrapped in metal braces, knew it was natural.

Her eyes, a gray shade between smoke and fog, gleamed like polished sterling in the candlelight as she walked into the bedroom on a predatory feline glide that was impossible to resist.

"Do you know how long I've been waiting for this moment?" she purred, snaring him in the silver web of her sultry gaze. Her voluptuous lips turned upward in a knowing smile. "Forever," she answered her own question.

Michael's heart was thundering painfully in a way he remembered all too well. The fact that he knew she was acting did not diminish one iota her mesmerizing sexual appeal.

Her eyes locked on his. Then, with tantalizing slowness, she slid one thin satin strap off her shoulder.

He swallowed painfully as the second strap followed the first. The nightgown slid down her body like an ivory silk waterfall, puddling on the white carpeting at her feet.

And then, although he had no idea where she'd hidden it, considering the clinging nightgown had revealed every feminine curve and hollow, she pulled out a blued steel pistol.

"I'm sorry, darling. It's nothing personal. But business *is* business."

Regret touched her remarkable eyes as she pulled the trigger.

*Fade to black.*

"Damn." Michael scowled at the television screen. What the hell was the matter with him? He'd never thought of himself as a masochist, yet when it came to Lorelei Longstreet, he was, apparently, a glutton for punishment.

It had been a decade since he'd seen her in person, longer still since he'd held her in his arms and tasted those full sweet lips. But as he watched the video of *Hot Ice*, her most recent blockbuster, it was impossible not to consider what might have been.

What would have happened, he wondered, if he'd gone to Los Angeles with her all those years ago? Would they have gotten married, as she'd so often fantasized out loud about? Would he have been able to watch her voluptuous body grow even rounder with his child?

Would Lorelei have still become one of the brightest stars in the Hollywood firmament? And more to the point, since he'd always believed her stardom inevitable, would she have continued to love him? If she ever had.

That thought was not a pleasant one. He polished off the beer he'd been drinking with the take-out pizza.

"She did love me." For a man who'd been accused of possessing an annoying amount of self-confidence, where Lorelei was concerned, Michael was remarkably unsure of himself. "As much as a young girl could love," he amended with a characteristic blend of self-honesty and pragmatism.

He'd been eighteen, Lorelei—who'd skipped her third and fifth grades to graduate high school early— a mere sixteen when they'd parted. She'd sobbed inconsolably, begging him to accept the baseball scholarship that would allow him to attend college with her in Los Angeles. But that would have meant leaving his mother alone to try to deal with his two younger—and trouble prone—brothers.

As much as he'd loved the stunningly beautiful young girl, as much as his heart had broken as he'd watched Lorelei's plane grow smaller and smaller, taking her away from him, he had felt compelled to stay and try to fill the role of man of the family in place of his globe-trotting, Pulitzer-prize-winning photojournalist father.

They'd been too young, of course. Distance and time had inevitably done their teenage romance in. But though he'd been involved with other women since then, there was an intrinsic part of his heart that would always belong to the first girl he'd ever loved.

The girl who had, in their years apart, become the quintessential ice goddess, a coolly sexy blonde reminiscent of a Hitchcock heroine.

"It wouldn't have worked," Michael repeated the words he'd been telling himself for years.

HALF A CONTINENT away, the object of all his frustration was not feeling like one of America's most idolized stars. The location shoot in Santa Monica was turning into a nightmare.

At first, despite the additional security that had been hired a determined fan had managed to get past the guards to hand her a ten-page love poem—written with a leaky pen on notebook filler paper.

Not only had he ruined her best take on the scene where her character—a reclusive mystery writer whose life has begun to mirror her murder novels—leaps off the end of the famed pier to escape her threatening stalker, the man's strange, manic behavior had frightened Lorelei.

Although it was the first week of August, the ocean water was still cold and by the third take, she'd begun to question her insistence on doing her own stunts. To make matters worse, her director, perfectionist Eric Taylor, apparently believed if one take was good, ten were even better.

"Cut!" Taylor called finally. "We're losing the damn light."

"Cut," the assistant director echoed.

"It's about time," Lorelei muttered as the wardrobe lady rushed forward with a towel and an oversize sweatshirt. Thanking the woman, she pulled the sweatshirt over her wet dress—which was clinging seductively, but icily to her body—and headed toward her trailer to change.

"You know," a deep voice offered, "I never realized that blue could be such an attractive skin color."

She flashed a mock scowl at the man sitting on the sidelines, a portable computer on his lap. "You realize, of course that this is all your fault. Surely you could have thought of some other way for her to escape her stalker?"

"Lots of ways," Brian Wilder, the film's screenwriter, answered without missing a beat. "But this was the best way to get you wet."

"Heaven forbid we disappoint all those adolescent males out there in the audience."

He laughed. "I didn't write this script for the kids." He waggled his blond brows in a roguish way. "Believe me, sweetheart, the sight of you in that wet dress is bound to send the opening weekend box office receipts soaring into the stratosphere."

Despite her physical discomfort, Lorelei smiled. Brian was one of Hollywood's golden boys. Although he was only in his early thirties, he was in demand by every producer in town, was a millionaire several times over, had the requisite sprawling mansion in Bel Air, the beach house in Santa Barbara and a ranch in the San Fernando Valley.

He was also, according to *Cosmopolitan* magazine, the most eligible bachelor in Hollywood. This was the fourth movie they'd worked on together and from what Lorelei could tell, fame and fortune hadn't gone to his head.

"It's so nice to have one's work appreciated," she drawled, wrapping her arms around herself.

She felt like one gigantic goose bump, her teeth were beginning to chatter, and there was no way she was going to be able to get home in time for a hot bath before her dinner date. A date where she planned to tell the owner of a trendy Beverly Hills restaurant she'd been seeing for three months that nothing was going to come of their relationship.

"You're a dynamite actress, Lorelei," Brian said, his expression turning momentarily serious. "But as your character pointed out in *Hot Ice*, business *is* business. This is a bottom line industry, sweetheart, and with that Venus de Milo body, you can't expect people to concentrate on your Shakespearean skills."

His words were, unfortunately, all too true. She knew she had done a good job of playing the revenge driven cat burglar in *Hot Ice*, and wished it mattered more to her fans than her scantily clad body.

"I'm thinking of giving it up." She regretted blurting out the thought that had been teasing her mind for months the moment she heard the words escape her mouth.

His expressive brow climbed his tanned forehead. "You're kidding."

Now that she'd said it, she couldn't see any way to easily backtrack. "I said I was *thinking* about it. I didn't say I'd decided."

"What would you do?"

"Lots of things," she said airily, not wanting to mention the script she'd been writing and rewriting for nearly a year. It was a bittersweet coming-of-age teenage love story that admittedly mirrored her own long-ago failed romance. "It's not as if I'm in danger of starving anytime soon."

He tilted his head, studying her thoughtfully. "You're just cold," he decided. "And tired. You've been working too hard lately. Although I hate to say this, since I have a dynamite story tailor-made for you that I'd planned to pitch to the studio when we get back from shooting in New Orleans, you need a break."

He wasn't telling her anything she hadn't told herself.

"What I need," she said with a quick, quirky grin that was at odds with her cool blond looks, "is to get into some dry clothes before I catch my death of pneumonia." She patted his cheek. "I can see the tabloid headlines now: Actress turned into Popsicle. Hotshot screenwriter's action-packed script blamed for tragic demise."

He laughed, as he was supposed to. Then returned to his computer. Unfortunately, she'd come to recognize that intense expression; there'd undoubtedly be a stack of revised pages waiting in her dressing room when she arrived at work tomorrow morning.

As Lorelei peeled off her wet clothes in the cramped trailer, changing into jeans and a T-shirt for the drive home, she wondered what had ever made her believe that movie making would be a glamorous profession.

THE MAN SAT alone in the dark, watching the television screen as Lorelei rushed to change clothes again after a hurried shower, opting for a simple silk sheath that couldn't conceal the shapely body underneath. Her bedroom, decorated in the same pale foam green as her dress, was a sea of cool serenity. The man knew she was a great deal more passionate than appearances suggested.

He watched her run the silver-backed brush through her long straight hair, then enjoyed the sight of her short skirt rising up in the back as she leaned toward the mirror to smudge the charcoal eyeliner that was several shades darker than her gray eyes. A woman who'd choose those lace-topped stockings over panty hose was a woman who'd enjoy the more sensual side of life. A woman with a deeply erotic nature.

Lorelei Longstreet was every bit as alluring as the mythological sirens of the river Rhine for which she'd been named. And after months of watching and waiting, she would soon be his.

That thought, as always, made the man smile. As she applied a cotton candy pink gloss to her full, impossibly seductive lips, he wrapped the length of clothesline around his hand and imagined tying it around Lorelei Longstreet's slender white wrists.

LORELEI WAS RELIEVED when the shooting returned to the studio back lot the following week. Although she'd never considered herself the nervous sort, she had to admit that recent events had made her more cautious. More aware of the dangers that came with celebrity.

She was sitting in her dressing room, eating her usual lunch of sliced hothouse tomato and half a cup of cottage cheese when there was a knock on her door.

"Delivery for you, Ms. Longstreet," one of Eric Taylor's plethora of assistants called in to her.

She opened the door, thanked the young man, and began to open the envelope, assuming Brian had sent her another set of revisions.

Instead of the computer printed pages she was expecting, the package contained a single white envelope. The moment she saw her name typed on the outside of the envelope, Lorelei's blood turned cold. She ran to the door, but the assistant had already disappeared into the cavernous building.

She slammed the door, leaned back against it, then closed her eyes, willing her heart to stop pounding and her mind to clear. Unfortunately, the brief exercise was proving less helpful each time she was forced to employ it. Lorelei's hands were trembling as she picked up the phone and dialed the all-too-familiar number of the Los Angeles police department.

Less than twenty minutes after she placed the call, Detective Matt Gerard arrived on the scene.

"You didn't open it?" His grim expression echoed the dark dread the envelope had invoked.

"No. I remembered what you told me about not harming the evidence." Hating the way her professionally trained voice wavered, she didn't add that she'd feared reading whatever the man who insisted upon calling himself her "most devoted fan" had written this time.

"Good girl."

Since he'd worked hard on the baffling case, Lorelei didn't take offense at the detective's chauvinistic words. Instead, she watched as he carefully slit the end of the envelope, and managed to remove the single sheet of paper inside without touching the flap, where, if experience were any indication, the lab wouldn't be able to find any fingerprints.

"'My darling Lorelei,'" he read from the typewritten text out loud. "'Your work on location in Santa Monica was your best yet, though it broke my heart to see you so chilled. I watched the goose bumps rise on your arms, saw the way your nipples pebbled with the icy cold from the water, and thought of all the ways I'd love to warm you up.'"

Feeling goose bumps rise on her skin again, Lorelei desperately hoped the writer would refrain from going into detail. Unfortunately, her hopes were dashed and she was forced to listen to the sexually explicit fantasies of a disturbed mind. Although she'd love to shut her own mind to the onslaught of unnerving words, the detective had assured her that it was important to pay close attention to everything the man wrote in case he'd let slip a clue to his identity—some small seemingly inconsequential detail only she could recognize.

"'I fantasized about tying you to the tall, slender columns of your bed,'" Gerard read in his unemotional baritone, "'imagined watching us together in the full-length mirror on the back of your closet door.'"

He looked up at her with dark eyes that always reminded her of a depressed bloodhound. "He's been inside the house."

"Obviously." Her mouth had gone dry; Lorelei swallowed painfully. "My housekeeper left a note for me last week. Apparently a man came by from the cable company to check the signal."

"And she let him in?"

"It wasn't as if she were being careless," Lorelei defended her longtime employee. "I'd asked her to call about the snow I've been getting on the lower channels. She wouldn't have let anyone enter the house without showing proper credentials."

"Credentials can be forged," he muttered. "Hell."

Gerard seemed to take the illegal entry personally. The past two months had given Lorelei the impression that he was the kind of old-fashioned cop that truly cared, and after decades in the crime business, the detective had managed somehow to keep from burning out. Nevertheless there were times when she found him nearly as difficult to deal with as her stalker.

"If you had your way, I'd lock myself in my house, never go to work, not answer the phone, and shoot anyone who showed up at my gate. I wouldn't even be able to order a pizza."

He skimmed a momentarily nonprofessional gaze over her body, clad in jeans and a white T-shirt. "I have difficulty believing you eat that many pizzas."

Once again his detective instincts proved right on the money. Lorelei couldn't recall the last time she'd tasted a pepperoni.

"That's beside the point." She tossed her head, welcoming the tinge of irritation that managed to curb her earlier fears. "I was referring to the fact that you'd like to put me under house arrest until this man is caught."

"Just because a law is on the books doesn't keep the sicko creeps from stalking," he proclaimed succinctly. "And it doesn't stop them from killing."

His words hit too close for comfort. "I know." She sighed. "This is just so frustrating. And frightening."

"You're smart to be frightened. It'll keep you on your toes." He returned his attention to the letter. "'I imagined the fear and anticipation in your eyes as I cut off your nightgown—the sea green one that matches your bedroom walls and—'"

"Oh, my God." Lorelei interrupted, drawing in a quick, harsh breath.

"What's wrong? It'd make sense, if he's been in your bedroom that he'd go through your clothes—"

"No," she cut in again. "You don't understand. I had dinner with friends last night. Nothing special, just a small group of women who get together once a month. Last night was my birthday.... They gave me a gift."

"Tell me it wasn't a nightgown."

"A sea green one I'd mentioned lusting over from the Victoria's Secret catalogue. It was so lovely, I couldn't resist putting it on as soon as I got home."

He cursed. "The son of a bitch put a camera in the bedroom."

Knowing that this man who'd been watching her from the shadows for the past months had been observing her while she'd been sleeping, caused a frisson of fear to skim up her spine.

"That's it," he decided. "You're going to have to call off the trip to New Orleans."

"I can't do that." Even though a part of her knew the detective had a very good point, she'd always been a firm believer in the old theatrical saying about the show going on. "The summer fires forced us to switch location sites three times. We're already horribly behind schedule and—"

It was Gerard's turn to cut her off. "That's Taylor's problem," he said brusquely.

"True. But my name is on the marquee and the studio is threatening to take control away if Eric doesn't get it wrapped up by Labor Day.

"Besides," she said as a thought occurred to her, "I'd think that leaving town would be safer."

"Not if the guy follows you."

Good point.

"I'll contact the New Orleans Police Department," he decided. "Meanwhile, I'll send a lab team out to your house to get rid of the camera, or cameras, then dust for fingerprints, just in case."

"Do you think he might have left any?"

"No," he answered, crushing her faint hope. "But the equipment the guy's planted in your house might give us a clue, if it's unusual or technically advanced stuff. And we can always hope that the more he becomes fixated on his sick fantasies, the more likely he is to make a mistake."

"That's not exactly encouraging." Lorelei didn't really want to dwell on her stalker becoming even more obsessed.

"It's not my job to be encouraging. My job is to try to keep you alive. And to catch the damn weirdo before he crosses that thin line between fantasy and murder." He dragged a broad hand down his face. "We have learned one thing."

"What?"

"The guy knows about cameras."

"That's not unusual for this town."

"True. But it's something new. I'll want to talk with Taylor again. And everyone else working on your current film."

For someone who'd chosen to have her image portrayed on an oversize silver screen, Lorelei keenly guarded her privacy. Although she hadn't been able to keep her recent troubles a secret—the tabloids had gotten hold of the police report shortly after the first letter had arrived—she dreaded the idea of her work-mates being interrogated.

"Surely you don't suspect someone I work with?"

"It's my job to suspect everyone."

Although she guessed that was, indeed the truth, Lorelei also thought it was the most depressing thing she'd ever heard.

Despite the fact that Eric Taylor was always irresolute about whether to go with a first take while filming, he proved surprisingly decisive when he heard about the most recent letter.

"That's it," he said. "I'm going to do what I should have done in the beginning. Hire a bodyguard to watch you around the clock."

"That's not necessary." Lorelei repeated what she'd said the first time he'd brought it up.

"It's no longer your decision."

"It's my business. And my life."

"It may be your life you're behaving so cavalierly about, but it's become my business," he countered. "Since this film would shut down if anything happened to you before we wrap, I have a vested interest in that lush body of yours. Which means I'm willing to pay to have it protected."

"You have such a way with words," she muttered. Once again she was grateful for the flash of irritation that helped clear the clouds of lingering fear from her head.

"You want a writer, go find Wilder. I'm just a frazzled, overworked director trying to keep from having my film taken away by the frigging bean counters who have taken over all the studios these days."

He turned toward Gerard, who was leaning against the wall, his arms folded across his chest. "Would you explain to this hardheaded steel magnolia that a bodyguard is the perfect solution? Especially while we're shooting so many scenes on location?"

"Couldn't hurt," the detective agreed.

Although she'd been against the idea from the beginning, Lorelei secretly wished that he sounded a bit more positive about the plan.

# 2

A WEEK SPENT dealing blackjack on one of the riverboat casinos, looking for dealers who might be skimming from the profits, had left Michael's clothes smelling of cigarette smoke and his head jangling with the sound of jackpot alarms. He was looking forward to the relative solitude of his office.

He'd opened the detective agency after leaving the NOPD. Although he'd enjoyed his work as a homicide detective, he'd found himself embroiled in a political battle when the various business and tourist powers didn't want it known that a serial rapist turned killer had begun stalking the French Quarter.

He'd done his job and apprehended the killer, then, fed up with a system that would put dollars before innocent citizens, he'd walked away from the police department and opened up Blue Bayou Investigations. Since spending the rest of his life peeking into motel room windows in search of errant spouses had been unappealing, he'd decided to specialize in executive protection and company security.

Times being what they were, he had more business than he could handle. Which was one reason he'd been more than happy to take his brother, Shayne, on as a full partner.

Shayne, who'd recently returned to New Orleans after a decade of living a shadowy existence in the European espionage community, greeted him with a grin as he entered the office located above a French Quarter antique stop.

"I take it you got your man," he said.

"I always do. Although in this case it turned out to be a woman."

Michael swept a quick glance around. Although he and Shayne had been working together for nearly three months, he still couldn't get used to the changes. Before, the place had had a relaxed, lived-in appearance; these days it was neat and filled with high-tech computer equipment. And although Michael missed the clutter, he had to admit that the bookkeeping system Shayne had installed was solving a lot of problems.

He went over to the portable refrigerator, took out a bottle of beer, offered one to his brother, then popped the tops on both long-necked bottles.

Shayne took a swallow of the Dixie beer. "This is one thing I really missed all those years away from home," he said, eyeing the brown bottle with appreciation.

Michael took a drink from his own bottle. "I thought Europe was a beer drinker's paradise."

"Beer flows like water over there," Shayne agreed. "But the circles I moved in tended more toward Cristal champagne and Pouilly Fuisse."

"Must've been hard," Michael drawled, "playing the role of a jet-set playboy all those years."

Shayne's grin was the same self-satisfied one Michael remembered seeing the day his brother had beaten him on the dirt basketball court behind their uncle Claude's bayou cabin by revealing he'd finally taught himself to dunk.

"It's a dirty job," Shayne agreed, a sparkle of laughter in his eyes. "But somebody had to make the sacrifices it takes to keep America free."

"Sounds good to me."

Michael threw himself down on the sofa that had taken the place of the old one he'd found at a Garden District estate sale. Although he had to admit the glove soft black Italian leather contributed to an impression of success, he couldn't help missing the comfortable, raggedy overstuffed cotton-covered one.

He put his feet up on the scarred wooden coffee table he'd refused to let Shayne replace with a trendy glass-topped model—a guy had to put his foot down somewhere—took another drink and enjoyed the cool taste as it slid down his throat. It was summer in the city, and the humidity was like a hot damp curtain hanging over the French Quarter. The ancient air-conditioning system in the building was doing little more than moving the wet air around and his shirt was already sticking to his back.

Shayne, on the other hand, looked disgustingly cool in a white silk shirt. From his vantage point on the sofa, Michael couldn't detect a single wrinkle. No wonder his brother had been able to pull off that jet-set act for so many years.

Although Michael had always considered himself a

damn good undercover detective, he figured he'd be lucky to last a day playing the role of a filthy rich, devil-may-care playboy.

"Speaking of life-styles," Shayne said, "I'm a bit disappointed to discover that the life of a detective isn't exactly the way it's portrayed on television."

"Getting bored already?"

Michael wouldn't be surprised. Shayne, like their other brother Roarke, seemed to have inherited their famous father's wanderlust. Roarke, it seemed, had hung up his rambling shoes. In fact, he'd recently announced he was getting married on Labor Day to Daria Shea, a parish prosecutor.

Since Shayne was now involved with the agency's landlady, antique dealer Bliss Fortune, Michael had been hoping the youngest O'Malley brother might follow Roarke's lead.

Not that he'd miss him all that much if he did leave town. But their mother would. Hell, Michael admitted, that was a lie. He'd gotten used to having both his brothers back home in New Orleans. It was almost like old times, but with a lot less responsibility.

"I'm not at all bored," Shayne assured him. "If nothing else, attempting to follow the paper trail you laughingly refer to as an accounting system is keeping me more than busy.

"It's just that I envisioned us living like Thomas Magnum, with tons of gorgeous, willing women—hopefully clad in little more than bikinis and skimpy lingerie—throwing themselves at us. And paying a daily rate for the privilege."

"What do you want other women for? When you've got Bliss?"

The dancing devils left Shayne's pale blue eyes and his gaze turned thoughtful. "Good point." He took a longer pull on the bottle. "She's different," he admitted quietly.

"Special," Michael added. If he and Bliss hadn't started out being such good friends, he might have considered trying to get something going with the warmhearted antique dealer. But that was before Shayne had staked his claim on her.

Shayne sighed. "She is that."

Michael heard a *but* in his brother's voice. "Having troubles?" he asked casually.

"Nah." Shayne shook his head. "Not really. I've just got some stuff I have to work out in my own head."

"Just so you don't hurt her. Because if you do, even though you are my kid brother, I'd have no choice but to shoot you."

"Makes sense to me." The grin was back. This time more devilish than before. Michael, who'd witnessed it too many times over the years knew it foreshadowed some new scheme.

"What have you gotten yourself into?" he asked suddenly.

"Me?" Shayne placed a tanned hand against his pristine shirtfront. He was the only man Michael knew who could get his fingernails manicured and not look like some sissy jerk.

"See anyone else in this place? Don't try to dodge

the question. After all these years, I know every one of your tricks."

This time Shayne's sigh was deep and dramatic. "Oh, ye of little faith. I'm going to love watching you apologize for not trusting me."

Actually, the only two people in the world Michael did trust were his brothers. And, of course, his mother. But she wasn't the subject at the moment.

"But something's come up," he pressed.

"Actually, I did have an interesting call today," Shayne revealed, seeming more than happy to shift the conversation from his love life. "From a prospective client in Los Angeles. Seems he's coming to our fair city on business and was looking for a firm that could provide executive protection."

"He called the right place."

"That's exactly what I told him. Then, after assuring him that we're the best in the business, and stating our sterling credentials, I told him that we could possibly, if we did some juggling, fit his case into our busy schedule. For our usual rate of a thousand dollars a day. Plus expenses."

"A thousand bucks a day?" Michael put the empty bottle on the table beside his feet.

"Plus expenses," Shayne reminded him.

"That's more than double Blue Bayou's usual fee."

"True. But there are two of us now. Besides, Mike, this guy can afford it...and it'll help make up for that freebie you did last week."

"I suppose you could have turned the job down? The woman's husband snatched her kid, Shayne.

Right off the street in front of her house. And the police sure as hell weren't doing anything to find him."

"The little girl just happened to be the man's kid, too."

"The father's a drunk and a small-time crook. A judge decided the man didn't even deserve unsupervised visitation rights when he gave the mother sole custody."

"Too bad the judge didn't figure out a way for her to get some child support bucks out of the guy. So she could afford to pay a detective to find the kid."

"It cost a lot for her to come here from Pittsburgh, and besides, she had to take time off without pay from her waitressing job. I didn't see any point in making a bad problem worse."

"That's my big brother." Shayne lifted his bottle in a salute. "Saint Michael, defender of small animals, women and children."

"Sometimes you just have to help, whatever the cost," Michael grumbled, hating the slant the conversation had taken. Since when was it a crime to do a good deed?

"You're right," Shayne surprised him by agreeing. "And, if you want to know the absolute truth, I hope I would have done the same thing under the circumstances. However, the fact remains that we have rent to pay, food and beer to buy, not to mention New Orleans Saints season tickets to pay for. Which makes the Robin Hood method of billing appropriate in this case."

"So, we're going to rob from the rich to help the poor?"

"Do you have a better idea?"

"No," Michael admitted. "Like everything else you think up, it makes a certain skewed sense."

"Of course it does." Like his two older brothers, Shayne had never lacked in self-confidence. "Okay. Here's the deal. There's this movie company coming to town to shoot on location."

"And they want us to keep the gang-bangers from harassing them," Michael guessed.

"Uh-uh. This is a personal protection matter. Seems the star has attracted herself a stalker."

"In Los Angeles?"

"Yeah, but according to the detective who's been handling the case for LAPD, there's a chance the guy might be obsessed enough to follow her. I assured the director—his name's Eric Taylor, he's the guy who does a lot of those action thrillers—that you'd had experience with stalkers."

Too much, Michael thought grimly. The woman he'd once thought he might marry had been stalked twice by two different men. The second one had almost killed her. If he hadn't arrived at her house when he had...

"So," he said, putting grim thoughts of that Christmas day behind him, "who's the star we're going to be baby-sitting?"

"That's the cool part." Shayne's grin lit up the room even more than the bright southern afternoon sun streaming through the window. "It's an old friend."

A fist twisted at Michael's gut. It couldn't be, he assured himself. Although life was filled with coincidence, surely fate wouldn't play such a dirty trick.

"I assume this old friend has a name?"

Shayne leaned back in the high-topped leather chair that had cost more than Michael's first car. His expression was one of sheer satisfaction.

"None other than Lorelei Longstreet."

"I FOUND A DETECTIVE," Eric announced as he and Lorelei sat out on the balcony of her Malibu home.

Her neighbors were near enough that she could practically touch their houses by stretching out her arms, and when she'd first leased the beachfront house she'd been willing to trade privacy for the pleasure of having the ocean at her front door. Lately Lorelei had had reason to question that decision.

She ran her fingernail around the rim of her wineglass. "I really hate this."

"I know." His expression echoed his words. "And I know I've said that it's the budget I'm protecting, but the truth is, Lorelei, I'd never forgive myself if anything ever happened to you."

"Nothing's going to happen to me." She said it firmly, as if speaking the words could make it so.

"Not if I can help it."

A little silence settled over them. Lorelei watched a young man running at the edge of the sun-sparkled water, accompanied by a golden retriever and envied the carefree appearance of both dog and man.

"So," she said, knowing there was no escaping the

topic until her stalker was apprehended, which hopefully would be sooner rather than later, "did you call the agency Detective Gerard recommended?"

"Yeah. Blue Bayou."

"Sounds nice." Too pleasant for a business dealing with potential killers, she thought.

"The guy I spoke with was friendly enough."

The director's drifting gaze caught sight of a young blonde in a thong bikini that barely covered the essentials. There'd been a time when Lorelei wouldn't have thought anything about his obvious knee-jerk reaction to the gorgeous, scantily clad woman. But her recent troubles had forced her to wonder if even a man she admired, as she did the director, could turn from interested male to obsessive stalker.

Eric sighed as he watched the woman embrace a buffed-up young man who was as handsome as she was beautiful. "Anyway," he said, turning back toward Lorelei, "this Detective O'Malley assured me that the agency has had successful experience with stalkers. Which backs up what Gerard told us."

"O'Malley?"

It couldn't be, Lorelei assured herself. New Orleans's population was filled with descendants of those early Irish who'd arrived in the delta country with broad backs and a willingness to work hard. Indeed, there'd been so many of them—a hundred thousand between the years of 1820 and 1860, she remembered from her schooldays—that they were considered more expendable than costly slaves and had been assigned the dangerous jobs of constructing the canals, levees, warehouses and bridges that had made New Orleans a thriving city of commerce.

"Shayne O'Malley," Taylor confirmed. "Sounded like a local, from his accent."

"Yes." She felt a headache threaten at the familiar name. So Shayne had grown up to be a detective. That made sense, she decided. He'd always been the flashiest of the three brothers; she could easily picture him living the life of a television action hero. Not that the scripted life of a TV detective bore much resemblance to the real thing, she reminded herself. "He is."

Taylor lifted a brow. "Do you know the guy?"

"New Orleans is a small town," she murmured. Indeed, she'd always thought it suffocatingly small, which had been one of the reasons she'd come to Los Angeles in the first place. "I knew the family."

"Small world."

"Isn't it?" She resisted, just barely, from rubbing her temples where the headache had begun to drum. She wanted to ask the all-important question, but she knew that nothing ever escaped the director's eagle eye, and she didn't want to give him insight into her personal life. Even one she'd successfully—at least most days—put behind her.

"Guess that means you know his partner, too."

His tone was casual, but his narrowed eyes revealed he'd caught the faint hitch in her tone and was interested. Terrific. The man might be incredibly talented, but his new wife—his third, or his fourth, Lorelei had given up keeping track—was one of Hollywood's worst gossips.

"I suppose that depends on who his partner is," she countered, using every bit of her acting ability to keep her tone as nonchalant as his.

"Apparently it's his brother."

"Roarke?" That made sense. The two younger O'Malley brothers had always had a great deal in common. They were both intelligent, dashing, and devil-may-care. She could easily imagine them going into business together.

"Uh-uh. Matthew, Mark, something biblical like that."

He wasn't fooling her for a minute. Lorelei knew the man had a virtual Rolodex tucked away inside his agile, perfectionist mind.

"Michael," she told him what he undoubtedly already knew.

"That's it. Like the archangel. I knew it was biblical."

He refilled his glass, topped off hers, then leaned back, crossed his legs and observed her with the unblinking eye of a man framing a shot. Which he undoubtedly was. Lorelei was all too aware of his habit of considering anyone's personal life nothing more than a script waiting to be filmed.

Indeed, he'd even profiled his own former drug use, his disastrous marriages and subsequent divorces in various movies that were little more than slightly altered autobiographies. His last wife had sued when he'd parlayed her treatment at the Betty Ford Clinic for alcohol abuse into a film.

"I went to school with Michael," she volunteered as

his silence lingered uncomfortably like morning fog that refused to burn off. "He also mowed our lawn for several years."

"Ah, the princess and the commoner." He nodded in a way that made her fear he was already concocting an idea to hand over to Brian Wilder for a screenplay. "Young love in the bayou. Hot, steamy, with lots of skin. Could be a winner with Generation X demographics."

She forced a laugh as the scenario proved too close for comfort. "Your imagination is running away with you again, Eric. We went to the same school, but Michael was older than I was. I hardly knew him." Now that was an out-and-out lie.

"Guess you didn't keep in touch after you came out here?"

"No." She'd been young and hurt and had believed, with all the conviction of a girl in love, that Michael would cave in to her tearful demands and follow her to California. Unfortunately, when that hadn't proven the case, she'd come to the reluctant conclusion that he didn't love her. At least not in the all-encompassing, heartaching way she loved him.

"Then I guess you didn't know he'd become a cop?"

Michael a cop? It fit, she decided. He'd always believed he knew best for everyone. He'd always had a deep-seated protective streak, which she'd resented all those times he'd refused to make love to her, insisting that she was too young to make such a life-altering decision. As a New Orleans police officer, he could take care of the entire city. Tell everyone what to do and have the badge to back up his demands.

She did not, naturally, share this thought with Eric. "And now he's a private detective?" she asked with studied casualness.

"Yeah. The brother—Shayne—explained that he'd been a homicide detective before that. Apparently he's had experience with stalkers. Including two cases where different guys were after a woman he was involved with. Some reporter at a local television news station."

"That's a high-profile career," Lorelei mused. "I can see where it might attract some undesirable attention."

"Kinda like being a movie sex goddess," Eric said.

"I'm guessing, since Shayne told you this, that Michael apprehended the stalkers."

"He said something about his brother always getting his man."

Despite her discomfort, Lorelei smiled. "Like Dudley Doo-right." When Eric gave her a blank look, she said, "You know, the cartoon Mountie who always gets his man."

"Oh, yeah." Eric sipped his wine. "Guess that'd make Desiree Dupree the guy's real-life Tess Trueheart."

"That's the news woman's name?" It was a lovely name. And vaguely familiar.

"Yeah. Although I don't know if she kept the last name when she married. She should have," he decided. "It's the kind of name that looks great rolling by in the credits. Better than Desiree O'Malley by a long shot."

It had been so many years since she and Michael had been together. So many years since she'd dreamed of a life with him. Lorelei told herself that she'd moved beyond that painful time, that Michael O'Malley no longer had the power to hurt her. But hearing the news that he'd married caused a cold wave of shock to wash over her. Followed by a tug of regret that pulled her beneath that icy wave like a riptide.

Like some crazy, near-death experience, scenes flashed before her eyes, changing and tilting like kaleidoscope facets, some sweet, some glorious, some so sad they made her eyes sting with unshed tears.

She had no idea how long she sat there, caught up in the grips of the past, but when she emerged from her dark undertow, she found Eric watching her with renewed interest.

"Something wrong?" he asked.

"No." The sea breeze blew a few strands of pale hair across her eyes; she brushed them back with a trembling hand.

It was over, Lorelei realized. Finally, truly over.

Which wasn't surprising. She couldn't have expected a man like Michael to wait forever. After all, his life was none of her business. It didn't hurt to discover he now had a wife named Desiree and perhaps even a house filled with children.

And maybe a dog. Didn't children always want dogs? She certainly had. Not that she'd been allowed one, of course, but if wishes had been puppies she would have had an entire kennel full.

She didn't care what Michael O'Malley was doing. Or who he was doing it with, Lorelei assured herself.

*Liar.*

# 3

LORELEI TOLD HERSELF that she should have expected
him. But Eric had told her that he'd made the arrange-
ments with Shayne, which had led her to believe that
the youngest O'Malley brother would be the one
meeting her at the airport. Instead, as she exited the
jetway, her gaze locked right on to Michael O'Malley.

Not that she could have missed him. He stood head
and shoulders above the gathered crowd awaiting
friends and loved ones at the gate. His hair, while
shorter than she remembered, was still as black as a
moonless midnight over the bayou and his eyes were
the deep blue of a tropical lagoon.

He'd always been physically strong, but in the years
since she'd last seen him, he'd definitely bulked up.
His obvious strength and the no-nonsense expression
on his ruggedly handsome face made her suppose
that he was a success in the personal protection business.

As she took in his broad shoulders, wide chest and
upper arms that reminded her of the sturdy limbs on
the five-hundred-year-old oak trees in her parents'
front yard, Lorelei experienced a hormonal burst that
felt as if an entire Fourth of July's worth of fireworks
had just exploded inside her.

The man's married, she told herself sternly. Which definitely made him off-limits. Reminding herself that she'd been the one who'd insisted on coming to New Orleans against Detective Gerard's dire warning, and realizing there was no way the studio was going to risk the location shoot without protecting their most expensive asset—namely their star—she pasted a polite smile on her face and firmly instructed her heart to stop its ridiculous pounding.

"Hello, Michael." A diamond tennis bracelet flashed on her wrist as she held her hand out to him. "What a pleasant surprise. I was expecting Shayne."

"Something came up," Michael said, as he took the slender silk-smooth hand in his. The something in question had been the threats he'd made to deter his brother, who was eager to be the one to meet their celebrity client.

"I hope there's no problem."

"Nothing we can't handle."

"Eric told me that you're partners," she said as she withdrew the hand he was still holding.

His touch on her elbow, leading her in the direction of the baggage claim area, was distinctly possessive. Lorelei considered shaking off the light touch, then decided not to start things out on a negative gesture.

"We've been partners for the past few months."

"I imagine you both carry guns?" She skimmed a sideways glance over the dark linen sport coat he was wearing over his polo shirt, wondering if he was wearing a shoulder holster beneath it. Or, perhaps he'd stuck a pistol into the back of his jeans, like a movie cop, she considered, disgusted with herself when the idea proved unreasonably exciting.

Michael braced himself for a Hollywood liberal antigun lecture. "It sort of comes with the job description. Guns are often helpful in the personal protection business."

"I'd imagine they would be," Lorelei agreed smoothly, ignoring the sarcasm in his tone. She bestowed a dazzling smile on a clutch of businessmen standing at a terminal bar trying to catch her eye. It was an automatic smile, the professionally flirtatious one she pulled out for public appearances. "I'm just a little amazed that neither of you has shot the other, yet."

He'd begun to seethe about that sexy, hot-as-hell smile she'd flashed at those leering businessmen. But as his mind backtracked, rerunning what she'd just said, Michael's irritation dissolved.

"We may have our little differences," he allowed, enjoying her dry joke, "but Shayne understands that while we may be partners, I'm still the boss."

"Still throwing your weight around?" She remembered youthful wrestling matches. There'd been times when Roarke and Shayne had teamed up and taken Michael on. She couldn't recall a single instance when the two younger brothers had emerged victorious.

"A guy's gotta use whatever weapons he has to stay on top."

His deep-throated chuckle was like the rumble of thunder over the delta and pulled unwelcome chords inside Lorelei.

The light mood evaporated as fast as it had arisen, replaced by a tension that hummed between them as they continued past the newsstands, take-out cajun food counters and souvenir stands displaying miniature bottles of tabasco sauce and various sizes of grinning plastic alligators.

Because of her habit of speaking her mind, Lorelei had always been considered a bit of an anomaly in Hollywood. Deciding that it would be best to lay all her cards on the table, she stopped walking and turned to look up at him.

"There's something I have to say, right off the bat."

"Shoot." Although he'd decided an apology for past sins was too much to ask for, Michael nevertheless braced himself for some defense of her youthful behavior.

"I was against this plan from the beginning. And I still don't like it."

"I see." Michael rubbed his jaw and looked down into her face. The white lines bracketing her lips hinted at a stress he hadn't detected in her voice. "Are we talking about the studio hiring a bodyguard to protect you? Or is it the fact that Blue Bayou—and especially me—got the job?"

"The first. I have nothing against you personally, Michael." That was a white lie, but there was no way she was going to admit how badly he'd broken her heart. "I just don't like the idea of giving up my privacy."

Michael hadn't garnered the highest case closure rate and best confession percentage on the NOPD without being able to read a suspect. She was good. Real good. But she was a liar, just the same. She wasn't prepared to admit it, but she was bothered by his reappearance in her life.

"Seems to me you gave up your privacy when you decided to become a movie star."

His drawled words carried an edge that gave Lorelei the impression that an actress was not much higher on Michael O'Malley's personal hierarchy of professions than the women who took off their clothes in the windows of Bourbon Street strip joints.

"What I do up on the screen has nothing to do with my personal life."

"You may like to believe that, but obviously, there's some guy out there who thinks differently."

When his lagoon blue eyes turned as stony as his rugged jaw, Lorelei forced a shrug, trying to ignore the familiar, burning pain behind her rib cage.

"He's probably not dangerous. You've no idea how many men write me letters of undying devotion." She thought back to that scrawled ode she'd had shoved into her hand during the Santa Monica shoot. "In fact, my secretary can't possibly pass on all the mail, but I probably get at least a dozen proposals a week. And even more propositions."

"That isn't surprising."

He had, after all, along with most every other male in America, watched *Hot Ice* more times than he could count. While her sexy cat burglar role might not get every man thinking about *marriage*, he doubted that

anyone could see her in that negligee without fantasizing about dragging her off to the nearest bed.

"But when you start talking about break-ins and
hidden cameras, some guy's gone beyond the pale."

Although the private security company Eric had
sent to sweep her house after the police had removed
the camera in her bedroom had assured her there
were no additional concealed lenses or recording bugs
in her house, Lorelei hadn't been able to sleep in her
bedroom since receiving that frightening letter.

"I suppose you have a point," she allowed.

"Of course I do. Which is why, as long as you're in
Louisiana, either Shayne or I, or someone we trust,
will be right by your side."

The idea of remaining in such close proximity to a
man who could make her feel as if she were sixteen
years old again was not necessarily a comforting one.

"Which means you'll be calling all the shots."

"That's the way it works in the private protection
business."

Travelers surged around them. Some, recognizing
Lorelei, shifted their gazes to the man towering over
her, as if trying to figure out whether he was someone
famous. Other harried passengers appeared irritated
at the roadblock they'd formed. Neither Michael nor
Lorelei noticed.

"What if I don't agree?"

"I suppose we have two choices. You can try to talk
your director into firing me—"

"I already tried that," she muttered. "Unfortunately, he was outrageously stubborn."

"He couldn't be as stubborn as me. Which brings me to my second option."

"And that is?"

"We can wrestle for it. Two out of three falls."

"That's no fair. You're stronger."

"You called that one right."

Surprised that he was actually beginning to enjoy himself, Michael skimmed a finger down the slope of her nose. He'd spent years telling himself that he was over her. Now, although not accustomed to second-guessing himself, he decided that he just might have been wrong.

Neither of them spoke as they waited for her luggage to arrive, although he did lift a brow when she handed him the baggage stubs.

"Something wrong?"

"I suppose I expected more."

"Ah." She nodded. "You were expecting, I take it, the glamorous Beverly Hills movie star laden down with designer trunks."

"I suppose that's close," he admitted.

"I'm sorry to disappoint you."

It was his turn to skim a glance over her, an openly masculine appraisal that irrationally made her wish she'd chosen something more glamorous, more sexy, than her usual traveling clothes of black jeans, white long-sleeved cotton shirt and sneakers.

"On the contrary," he drawled, his voice as rich as the pralines she'd seen for sale beside the plastic alligators, "I'm not at all disappointed, Lorelei. I always predicted you'd grow up to be a beauty." His smile was slow and wickedly seductive. "And you did."

As she felt herself beginning to drown in his dark blue eyes, alarms sounded. Having always admired Michael's integrity, she was forced to wonder what had happened to him during their years apart. What kind of man had he grown up to be? she wondered.

The Michael O'Malley she'd known and loved would never have looked at a woman with lust in his eyes when he had a wife at home. Lorelei felt torn between cold fury and profound disappointment.

"What about Desiree?" she asked. "Is she beautiful?"

"Desiree? How do you know about her?"

"People talk."

"Obviously Shayne told your director."

"Obviously." Her voice was ice, her gaze chilly.

She'd turned as rigid as one of the iron girders on the Huey P. Long Bridge. Lorelei had never been a particularly temperamental teenager—except on those occasions when he'd reluctantly refused to take the sex she'd so enticingly offered. Obviously, Michael thought with regret, her years living the glamorous Tinseltown life had changed her.

"Now that you bring it up, yeah, Desiree's beautiful. Inside *and* out," he tacked on significantly.

Now she was forced to wonder what type of woman he thought *she* was. Did he actually believe all the tabloid hype? Did he think, just because she so often portrayed a woman of loose morals in the movies, she'd actually go to bed with someone else's husband?

"You're a lucky man."

Once again her words were tinged with frost. He couldn't believe she'd actually resent his having been involved with another woman. What the hell had she expected him to do after she'd dumped him? Join an order of Trappist monks and embrace a life of celibacy?

"I'd say Roman's the lucky one," Michael responded after a long pause. He was getting angry, he realized. Her snotty tone had caused a temper he seldom allowed himself to acknowledge to begin to simmer.

"Roman?"

"Roman Falconer."

"The novelist?"

"That's him. He used to be parish prosecutor before he turned writer." Roman was also one of the few politicians Michael had respected. Even if he had, at one time, seriously considered arresting the guy for murder.

The baggage carousel finally came to rumbling life with a loud announcement buzz. Ignoring it, Lorelei combed a distracted hand through her hair. Once again Michael caught the glitter of diamonds and wondered if the bracelet had been a gift from a lover.

"I remember Roman. Actually, he was a neighbor." As had Desiree Dupree for a very brief time. Her rigid, hard-hearted grandmother had sent her off to boarding school in Europe before the young girl had had time to unpack her suitcases.

"Oh yeah. I'd forgotten that." Although he'd spent

every Saturday morning mowing the vast Longstreet lawn, Michael had never been invited to the privileged environs on a social basis.

"I don't understand," Lorelei said.

That made two of them. "Understand what?"

He was standing over her—hovering over her, actually—making her tilt her head a very long way back to look up at him. He was too close. Too distracting.

"What does Roman Falconer have to do with your wife?"

"My wife?" Michael was momentarily baffled. Then the missing pieces clicked into place, like the sevens on all those slot machines that had nearly deafened him in the casino last week. "You thought I was married to Desiree Dupree?"

"Aren't you?"

"Of course not." It was his turn to drag a frustrated hand through his hair. "Hell, Lorelei, what kind of guy do you think I am? I wouldn't tell a woman she was beautiful—even if she *was* drop-dead gorgeous—if I was married to someone else."

Lorelei felt the blood rush to her face. She tried to remember if they had earthquakes in Louisiana, feared they didn't, but wished for one anyway, to swallow her up along with her embarrassment. When the floor didn't open up beneath her Keds, she realized there was only one thing to do.

"It seems I owe you an apology."

Since her scent had been driving him crazy since she'd gotten off the plane, Michael decided to make her suffer. Just a little.

The way he continued to look down at her, with that unreadable, frustratingly neutral expression she suspected was a holdover from his cop days, was beginning to make her nerves hum and her stomach burn. Lorelei considered digging into her purse for the ever ready roll of antacids, but decided there was no way she was going to let him know how strongly he affected her.

She heard a murmured complaint behind her and without taking her gaze from Michael's steady one, moved a few inches to the left. As if attached by an invisible cord, Michael moved with her.

"Well?" She folded her arms across the front of her shirt. "Aren't you going to say anything?"

"I thought it was your turn. Weren't you about to apologize?"

Her chin jutted out. Her eyes sparked with a temper only this man had ever been able to ignite. They moved again, this time for a young couple who pulled two duffel bags from the carousel.

"Obviously, Eric was confused." When his only response was a lifted brow, she ground her teeth, making a silent apology to her parents, who'd spent a fortune on her youthful orthodontia. "He mentioned Desiree Dupree had been at the center of two of your cases."

Michael nodded. "He got that part right." The second time had been his last case as a NOPD major crimes detective.

"He also said something about the two of you living together."

"We did, for a time." He paused, wondering how much more to tell her. Wondering if she cared. And, more to the point, why it mattered to him that she did. "It didn't work out."

"Oh." Lorelei had thought she'd been in trouble when she'd exited the jetway and suffered that jolt of feminine awareness. Finding out that he was not married made the man even more dangerous. "I'm sorry."

"It was over a long time ago." It didn't hurt now because, despite how much he'd truly cared for the sexy newscaster, it hadn't hurt then. Only one woman had ever possessed the ability to break his heart. And unfortunately, she was standing too damn close for comfort.

Wanting—needing—to return to neutral ground, Michael turned toward the rotating carousel. "Are those yours?"

She dragged her gaze from his shuttered face to the suitcases he was pointing toward. "That's them."

The spell that had made them oblivious to anything but each other had been broken. He retrieved the bags, tucked them both under one arm, and as she walked beside him toward the terminal exit, Lorelei couldn't decide whether she was relieved or disappointed.

Although the crew was staying at the Fairmont, Michael had arranged for Lorelei to register under an assumed name at the Whitfield Palace Hotel.

"I doubt even you can keep my arrival in the city a secret," she said as they took the private VIP elevator to the top floor penthouse suite.

"That'd probably be impossible," he agreed. "But at least this way, once the filming stops at the end of the day, we've got you isolated from the rest of the crew."

"Are you suggesting my stalker could be someone I know? Someone I actually work with?" She was as shocked by the idea now as she'd been when Detective Gerard had first suggested it.

"Could be." He stopped watching the numbers flash above the door and looked down at her. "I'm surprised Gerard didn't bring it up."

"He did," she admitted reluctantly. "But I assured him that he was wrong."

"And he dropped it?"

"He didn't share his investigation with me, but I received the impression that he was willing to trust my instincts."

"Somehow I doubt that. I'd guess that since he's obviously got a heavy caseload, it was easier just to hand you over to me."

"My case," she reminded him archly, bristling as he'd expected. "Nobody hands *me* over to anyone."

"Point taken." He would not, Michael vowed, allow either her seductive scent or her prickly independence to stop him from doing his job. "But since more than a few men working on this project fit a suspect profile, I'm not taking any chances."

"I don't believe this." She put her hands on her hips and stared up at him. "Name one."

"I can do better than that. But I suppose we can start with John Nelson."

"John?"

"As director of photography, the guy has the technical know-how to set up that rig in your bedroom."

"He might have the knowledge. But he'd never do it. Besides, John would be the last person on the crew to be interested in me in *that* way. He just happens to be gay."

Michael did not appear to be surprised by that little newsflash. "He also has an unfortunate addiction to playing the horses at Hollywood Park and is in debt up to his eyeballs to his bookies."

Lorelei had known about the gambling; it would have been impossible not to notice the tout sheets and phone calls. "Even if he *is* in financial difficulty, what would that have to do with me?"

"How much do you think the tabloid rags—or better yet some porno production company—would pay for film of you in the buff?"

She shuddered, felt the headache hum and the acid burn and giving up all pretense of cool composure, pulled the roll of Tums from her purse and chewed two of them. Then a third for extra measure.

"He'd never do that," she insisted. "We're friends. In fact, he even offered to let me stay with him last winter after my house was flooded by a storm."

He shrugged. "It would have been easier to get the shots in his own place."

Her response to that was an earthy curse that never would have escaped the teenage Lorelei's lips. The elevator dinged as it reached the top floor.

"That still doesn't explain why he'd suddenly turn stalker."

Michael didn't answer, frustrating her further. "I don't like this," she muttered as the steel doors slid open.

"That makes two of us."

The doors opened directly on to a marble-floored foyer. The walls were draped in a muted ivory-striped silk, the frame on the oversize mirror was tastefully gilded without being overly ornate, the furniture was neoclassical. As she stepped out of the elevator, Lorelei was surrounded by the heady fragrance of peach roses, pink gladioli, and white lilies.

"I was referring to you investigating my friends."

He shrugged as he pulled the electronic key out of his jacket pocket and inserted it into the slot on the door at the far end of the foyer. "I would have checked out your enemies, but amazingly, you don't seem to have any."

"I could have told you that."

Once again her sharp tone slid right off him like August rain off a duck's back. "Except, of course, the guy who's been stalking you." He opened the door, stepped back, and gestured her into the suite. "We'll discuss the rest of the crew over a late supper."

"I don't normally eat supper."

"You should. As terrific as you look, you could use a bit more meat on your bones. However," he continued, ignoring her sharp, angry intake of breath, "I do, as a rule, eat supper and since I spent an hour waiting for your delayed flight to arrive, I'm hungry enough to eat a gator."

"Perhaps the chef will run out and capture one for you," she said with feigned sweetness.

"That's an idea," he said easily. "But I'm willing to settle for a double cheeseburger. Despite its five-star billing, the Whitfield has the best burgers in town. And the fries are nearly as good as the ones you can get at The Port of Call."

"I don't eat meat any longer." She didn't add that she couldn't remember the last time she'd indulged in a French fry. It wasn't always easy being a sex goddess.

"Figures." He shrugged. "I guess you can just sip mineral water or champagne, or whatever movie stars drink while I eat, then."

His words brought her low seethe to a hot simmer, and Lorelei was about to let Michael know, in no uncertain terms, exactly how annoying she found his chauvinistic behavior, when his next words stopped her in her tracks.

"And while we're at it, you can give me the names of all the guys you've slept with in the past six months."

# 4

BEFORE LORELEI COULD destroy Michael with a few well-chosen words, a faintly familiar man stood up from a brocade couch, his smile warm and far more welcoming than any she'd received from Michael thus far.

"Hello, angel." Without asking permission, Shayne wrapped his arms around her. "It's about time you decided to come back from Lotus Land."

Recognition immediately dawned. "Hello, Shayne." His warm hug was highly unprofessional, but managed, just barely, to ease a bit of her irritation. "It's good to be back." She smiled up at him, unsurprised that the devil-may-care boy she remembered had grown up to be a devastatingly handsome man. "At least it was, until Michael decided to give me the third degree."

Shayne laughed and skimmed a hand down her cheek. Although the gesture, like the hug, was more than a little intimate, Lorelei couldn't help noticing his touch didn't affect her in the same way his brother's had.

"That's his specialty. When I first showed up back in town, he pointed a gun on me."

"Perhaps that had something to do with my catching you breaking into my building with a gun in *your* hand," Michael suggested dryly.

Although he believed Shayne's assertion that he'd given up his playboy ways when he'd fallen in love with Bliss Fortune, Michael damn well didn't like the sight of Lorelei wrapped in his brother's arms. Nor did he like the dazzling smile she was tossing back up at Shayne.

"Really?" Lorelei amazed and irritated Michael by laughing at that. Michael had yet to find a single humorous thing about the incident that could have ended up getting them both killed. "You always were incorrigible."

Michael felt like punching Shayne when he laughed right along with her. There was none of the tension between the two of them he'd felt earlier in the airport or during the nearly silent, twenty-minute drive to the hotel. It was as if the intervening years had never happened, as if they were kids again, hanging out on a lazy summer afternoon.

"It's a long story," Shayne said.

"Somehow that doesn't surprise me. And I can't wait to hear all about it. Although I doubt if I'll believe a word, since you were always the worst liar in the O'Malley family. Probably the entire state of Louisiana." She laughed again and shook her head. "And now you and Michael are partners. Amazing."

"There are days when I can hardly believe it myself," Shayne assured her. "But it's true." His boyish grin sparkled in the pale blue eyes that swept admiringly over her uplifted face. "You know, I thought I was giving up the high life when I came back to Louisiana. Who could have imagined I'd get lucky enough to guard the most gorgeous woman in Hollywood?"

Her lips turned down in a mock moue. "Michael thinks I'm too skinny."

Lorelei's complaint invited his practiced male gaze to zero in for a longer, more critical look. "I sure don't see any grounds for complaint."

"Thank you." She shot a victorious look over her shoulder at Michael. "He also wants a list of all my lovers."

"Ouch." Shayne looked at Michael with surprise. "You don't pull any punches, do you, big brother?"

"In case the two of you have forgotten, this isn't a social visit. We've been hired to protect Lorelei. Not feed her feminine ego, which undoubtedly gets enough strokes as it is from adoring fans."

Shayne cringed at the gritty words and tone while Lorelei began to simmer anew. Promising to meet them after tomorrow morning's shoot in Saint Louis Cemetery Number One, he gave Lorelei another hug and left the suite.

Once again an uncomfortable silence settled over Lorelei and Michael. Refusing to be intimidated, Lorelei was the first to break it.

"Didn't you say something about eating a gator? Or a cow?" She waded through the thick carpeting to the phone, plucked the receiver from the cradle and held it out to him. Her smile, which had bestowed such warmth and pleasure on Shayne, was blatantly feigned. "Perhaps you'll be in a better mood once you've had that cheeseburger."

Personally, Michael doubted that.

As he placed the room service order for a bacon double cheeseburger, sides of fries and slaw, and chicory coffee, he decided that the movie star he'd agreed to baby-sit was turning out to be a royal pain. Obviously, he was going to earn every cent of the outrageous fee Shayne was charging the studio.

Lorelei was tempted to order the most expensive champagne on the room service menu, but decided it would be a childish gesture. In the end she settled for a pot of tea, then went into the adjoining room to hang up her clothes while they waited for the order to arrive. Seeming determined to stay by her side, Michael followed.

"I do hope you plan to give me some privacy?" Negligently, she pulled a stack of lingerie out of the smaller bag and tucked it away in the top drawer of a very good antique reproduction of a Queen Anne walnut chest. "Although that tub is admittedly large enough for two, I'm not accustomed to sharing a bathroom."

The sight of all that lace and satin frippery made his mouth water. When he found himself fantasizing about unfastening the scarlet-as-sin bra, Michael knew he was in deep trouble.

With a mental shake, he rid himself of the tempting vision and brought his mind back to her question. "I only join women in the bathroom when invited."

"How reassuring." She smiled easily. "And since

I'm not in the habit of sleeping with the help, I suppose we have no problem."

"Did anyone mention sleeping?"

She tossed her hair back. "I was speaking figuratively."

"So was I." His grin, the first he'd given her, was quick and wicked and all too memorable. For a fleeting moment Lorelei wondered why she'd mistakenly thought Shayne was the more handsome brother.

Shayne O'Malley brought to mind those European jet-setters who populated the sunny beaches of Cannes during the annual film festival. He exuded a Cary Grant or James Bond type of sophistication she suspected most women would find irresistible.

But Michael—ah, she mused, feeling her blood pressure rise—Michael O'Malley was sex in the raw. He reminded her of some Renaissance statue. But not marble. Marble was too smooth. Too finished. This man could have been carved from an enormous piece of rough-textured granite. Although he'd undoubtedly shaved this morning, his stony jaw was already darkened with a blue-black shadow. His mouth was full and firm and appeared ruthless, even when he allowed one of those rare smiles.

"Well." She tossed her head. "So long as we understand each other, we shouldn't have any problem."

"None at all."

There was a knock on the adjoining door. As he went to admit the room service waiter, Michael was forced to consider that, although he had the scars to prove he'd survived a lot more trouble than a single

110 pound woman could possibly represent, Lorelei might just be the greatest challenge of his career.

She heard the door open, a murmur of voices, the squeaky wheel of a serving cart, the door closing again. When the unmistakable scent of fried fat wafted into the room, her stomach actually growled.

Not that she was hungry, Lorelei assured herself as she tossed the red lace bra and matching panties into the drawer. Then, knowing that she had no choice, she returned to the living room to resume the inquisition.

She'd stayed in Whitfield Palaces all over the world and knew them to be the epitome of luxury. Indeed, the slogan of the international chain was When Deluxe Will No Longer Do. Since the company was based in New Orleans, making this the flagship hotel, she was not surprised by the snowy white linen, heavy sterling and crystal that accompanied Michael's burger and fries. A Waterford vase with a bloodred rose claimed the center of the small table.

Michael took off his jacket, hung it on the back of the chair, then lifted the metal cover off the plate and eyed the burger with a look of lust Lorelei was accustomed to having directed at her. "What did I tell you? Terrific…. Sure you don't want some?"

She dragged her gaze from the leather shoulder holster his jacket had hidden to the oversize hunk of meat and kaiser roll filling the plate. "I told you, I don't eat meat."

"How about shellfish?" He poured a cup of tea from the porcelain pot. "You can't come to *Norluns*—" he drawled it in the native way she hadn't heard for years "—without indulging in some oysters or craw-fish étouffée."

Lorelei hadn't realized taste buds had memories. All it took was the mention of two of her favorite dishes to start her salivating. "Cajun food is so fatten-ing." Murmuring her thanks for the cup of tea he ex-tended toward her, she sat down on the corner of the couch.

"That's what's good about it. That and the hot sauce."

She couldn't argue with that. "I have to watch my weight. The first time I saw myself up on that huge screen, I felt enormous—like Gulliver in the land of the Lilliputians."

"You were undoubtedly the only person in the world who felt that way." He remembered almost swallowing his tongue when the camera had first ze-roed in on her, rising out of a sun-sparkled blue swim-ming pool like Venus on her half shell, her long plati-num hair tangling like wet seaweed over her shoulders.

Lorelei shrugged, trying to ignore the enticing aroma of melted Monterey Jack cheese. "The camera adds pounds. As Brian Wilder pointed out last week, I'm not being paid for my Shakespearian talents."

"Wilder." He took a bite and chewed thoughtfully. "The screenwriter."

"That's him. And he doesn't gamble."

"Nor drink or do drugs," Michael agreed. "In fact, from what I could dig up, despite his swinging bachelor image, the guy's so squeaky clean he doesn't even seem to jaywalk."

His obvious disbelief irked Lorelei. "Not everyone breaks the law."

"That's your opinion." He dipped a French fry into a dish of ketchup·and popped it into his mouth.

"But not yours."

"Honey, I've been around the cop business long enough to know that there's no such thing as a totally law-abiding citizen."

"Really?" She smiled coolly over the rim of her cup. "Well, for your information, Mr. Law and Order, you just happen to be looking at one."

Michael didn't immediately respond. Instead he picked up the heavy fork, scooped up a serving of slaw and gave her a long, probing look as he chewed.

"Say a clerk gives you back the wrong change," he suggested. "What do you do?"

"Point out the mistake, of course."

"How about taxes? Surely a rich lady like you must have fudged a bit on the bottom line?"

"I have a good accountant." She refused to be intimidated by his steady gaze. "He's well paid to find legitimate deductions—"

"Loopholes."

She lifted her chin. "Deductions. Don't forget, I appeared in that remake of Al Capone's story. The fact that the IRS guys were the only feds who were ever able to convict him sunk in."

"Cheating on your taxes is a national sport. But it's for chumps," he agreed. "How about speeding?"

"How about it?"

Another French fry, dripping with thick ketchup, stopped on the way to his mouth as he heard the hesitation in her voice. Lorelei could practically see the Gotcha! sign light up his dark blue eyes.

"You've been known to fudge on the limit." It was not a guess.

Her smile was practiced, designed to disarm. "Are you saying that all those white-and-black signs along the freeway aren't suggested speeds, Officer?"

"I'm saying that next time you get sent to traffic school, you might want to take in one of the comedy ones. I hear they're a riot."

Her eyes narrowed. "You actually had the gall to check *me* out?"

"Sure." He popped the fry into his mouth and chewed with such relish she was tempted to slug him.

"Surely you didn't suspect me of stalking myself?"

"Now that you bring it up, the thought did occur to me."

"What?" She caught herself before she could sputter. "I can't believe even you would be so cynical."

"Not cynical. Thorough. You're currently making a film about a woman who's being stalked. The movie happens to have run over schedule and over budget—"

"That's not my fault."

"I didn't say it was," he said, undeterred by her interruption. "However, the fact is that Eric Taylor, the man who called the cops in the first place, is also on the verge of having the guys in the Armani suits in the executive offices take control away from him.

"If something happened to garner a lot of publicity—let's say that life started imitating art—well, hell, even a guy like me who doesn't know anything about the movie business could guess that would boost the potential audience right through the roof."

"I would never, ever, agree to participate in such a ridiculous scheme."

He shrugged and reached for his coffee. The porcelain cup looked small and fragile in his large hands. "I don't remember accusing you of that."

"But you implied it."

"If I have something to say, Lorelei, I say it. I don't imply. Yeah, I think that some actresses might do anything for publicity. And although you're not as snowy white as you first tried to make me believe, a lead foot on the gas pedal of that sporty little Mercedes convertible you bought last year doesn't mean you'd try to manipulate the police to garner a few extra minutes on 'Entertainment Tonight.'"

"Thank you."

"You're welcome. But just because I don't consider you a suspect doesn't mean that the scenario isn't workable."

"Eric wouldn't do that."

"You're sure."

"I'd stake my life on it."

"You realize, of course, that may be exactly what you're doing."

Angry at him for remaining calm while doing such

a bang-up job of jangling *her* nerves, Lorelei jumped to her feet. "This is ridiculous! The man, whoever he is, is obviously obsessed. But I can't believe he'd want to kill me. He says he loves me."

"He wouldn't be the first guy to attempt to love a woman to death."

His expression, rife with grim memory, cooled her fury. "You're talking about Desiree," she guessed.

"Yeah." He dragged a hand down his face, recalling how close the woman who'd been his lover and had remained his friend had come to being killed by the French Quarter rapist. "The first guy was sick, but although I was more than happy to send him away, I still believe he was pretty harmless. All things considered."

"But the second?" she prompted quietly.

"He'd killed before." He hadn't been able to stop the murder of a teenage runaway. Michael figured that would always gnaw at him. "And he would have kept killing."

"If you hadn't stopped him."

"Yeah."

"Did you..." She paused, carefully framing her words as she realized that Eric hadn't given her the entire story. She glanced at the black leather holster. "Shoot him?"

"Yeah."

For a man who claimed to be outspoken, he definitely wasn't a font of information. "Did you kill him?"

"Someone had to."

Since she knew that Desiree was now married, Lorelei realized that the story had a relatively happy ending. Nevertheless, the fact that Michael had been forced to shoot to death the man who had stalked his lover, and the realization that she might face similar danger, made her suddenly go weak at the knees. She sank down onto a Queen Anne chair upholstered with birds and flowers.

For such a large man, Michael proved capable of quick action. One minute he was seated at the table, the next he was standing over her, his fingers splayed against the back of her head.

"Put your head between your knees."

"I don't need to—"

"Shut up," he said equably. "And do it. I'm being paid big bucks to take care of you, Lorelei. I'm not going to let you ruin my reputation by fainting on the first day."

"I never faint."

"Good for you. Let's keep it that way." He was pushing down, the pressure of his hand gentle, but determined. Since it was difficult to argue while little white dots were swimming in front of her eyes, Lorelei did as instructed.

Her vision gradually cleared.

"Feeling better?"

"A bit." Although her head was no longer spinning, his absently caressing touch was causing new havoc to her equilibrium.

"Here." He shoved a glass of water in front of her.

"You're probably dehydrated from the flight. Take a long drink."

"I'd forgotten how bossy you can be," she muttered. She was also mildly irritated when the ice water tasted better than the finest vintage French champagne.

"And I'd forgotten how stubborn you could be," he countered mildly. "You always were spoiled rotten, Lorelei." She'd been rich, beautiful, pampered, and he'd been crazy about her. "Obviously all those folks in Hollywood continued where your parents left off."

Lorelei had always felt a little guilty about the difference in their life-styles. Although Michael certainly wasn't poor—his father, she remembered, was a famous, prizewinning news photographer—she'd been born into wealth and privilege while he'd always seemed to be working. And trying to keep Roarke and Shayne out of trouble, which she suspected had been a full-time job all on its own.

She lifted her head the rest of the way and looked straight into his eyes. "I didn't get everything I wanted."

Her tone was soft, almost a whisper. But Michael heard her loud and clear.

He'd thought the ashes of their love affair had long gone cold. But as she looked up at him, and he looked down into those wide silver eyes, Michael could feel the stir of old embers warming.

"You're not alone in that." He returned to the table and began stacking some French fries onto a gilt-edged plate. "Here, you'll feel better if you eat something."

"I told you, I have to watch my weight."

"I'll make a deal with you. You eat enough to keep yourself from fainting and I'll watch your weight."

He might be bossy and chauvinistic, but Michael possessed a strong independent streak that made him so different from the men she knew. Men who spent so much of their time and energy playing Hollywood games.

"I have problems seeing you working on the police force."

"What's the matter? Don't I inspire confidence?"

Forgetting that she had no intention of eating the fries, Lorelei picked one up and absently chewed on it as she cocked her head and studied him. "Of course you do. But that's not the point. I just can't see you following orders."

"Neither could I." He shrugged and took another bite of fry himself. "That's probably why the brass didn't try too hard to keep me on the force."

"It was their loss."

He arched a brow. "Am I mistaken, or did a compliment just escape those petal pink lips?"

The lips in question curved. She felt both her mood and her spine loosen. "I suppose I've been a bit overly defensive."

"That's understandable, given the circumstances."

"Yes. Well." She took another bite of French fry that had been cooked to perfection—golden brown and crunchy on the outside, white and flaky on the inside. "It's not that I'm frightened—"

"You should be," he interjected in a neutral tone.

"I suppose so." She sighed again, then reminded herself that she had no intention of letting some sicko get the best of her. "However, since Eric has now hired the intrepid O'Malley brothers to baby-sit me, I'm going to let you and Shayne worry about the details."

"That's what we're getting paid for," he agreed.

"And very well, too, I hear."

He shrugged. "You're undoubtedly worth it."

She couldn't help smiling again at that. "Undoubtedly." Her expression sobered as she picked up another fry. "Could I have some ketchup with this?"

He put the dish on the tripod table beside the chair.

"It's the lack of control." The ketchup was thick and clung to the wedge of fried potato. When she popped it into her mouth, she detected the unmistakable fiery taste of tabasco sauce that invoked old memories of clandestine trips with Michael to his uncle Claude's bayou fishing cabin.

She took a drink of water to cool her tongue. "I've learned to live with the fact that there's very little control in the business I've chosen. But this..." She shook her head and grimaced. "This is my life we're talking about, Michael. I've worked hard to keep my personal life private. And he's invaded it."

"I know." Because he was struck by a sudden urge to pull her close, to stroke his hand down her back, to bury his lips into the silky fragrant slide of her hair, to bury another part of him into her tight warmth, Michael sat back down at the table and took a huge bite of the hot juicy burger that could not satisfy this new hunger.

"I won't let you down, Lorelei," he promised grimly.

He'd said those words to her a decade ago. The night before she'd flown to Los Angeles, the night he'd promised that they'd be married, make a home, have children. And then, by the time she'd come home for Thanksgiving, he'd conveniently forgotten her and the vows they'd made to each other one star-spangled moonlit night.

They'd both been young, she reminded herself. She'd been foolish to expect an eighteen-year-old boy, even one as responsible as Michael had been, to tie himself down to one girl. They'd moved on with their lives, as their parents—who'd been against the youthful romance in the first place—had predicted they would.

But now fate and some obsessed fan had brought Michael back into her life. And the twinges of desire she'd been feeling were definitely not for any handsome, serious boy.

She wasn't yet prepared to trust him with her heart. But she could, Lorelei knew, trust Michael O'Malley with her life.

"I'm going to get him, Lorelei," his deep voice broke into her contemplative silence.

She looked up at him, her tangled emotions in her eyes. "I know," she said, relieved to discover that she honestly believed that he would.

# 5

TO HER AMAZEMENT, Lorelei not only finished off the French fries, but the slaw as well. And she also only managed an impotent complaint when Michael had called down and ordered two servings of bread pudding.

"If I keep eating like this, the wardrobe woman's going to kill me," she said on a moan that was part regret and part pleasure.

"So you run a little more in the morning," he said with a shrug, enjoying the sight of her tongue licking the caramel whiskey sauce off the back of the spoon.

She wasn't surprised he knew about her morning exercise routine. A routine she'd stopped when the letters had escalated, opting instead for the safety of dancing along with an aerobics tape in her living room. "I'd have to run all the way to Baton Rouge and back to work this off."

"It's the Big Easy," he reminded her with a shrug. *"Laissez les bons temps rouler."*

"That's easy for you to say, since I have a feeling that it's not often that you let those good times roll," she said, hitting remarkably close to home for someone who hadn't seen him in over a decade. "Besides, you're not the one who's supposed to squeeze into a stripper's outfit."

"A stripper's outfit?" He frowned even as the idea proved personally appealing. It was bad enough that she sashayed around the set in lingerie. Once her stalker got a look at her in pasties and a G-string, all hell would break loose.

"If two Band-Aids and a sequined triangle the size of an eye patch can be called an outfit," she said.

Michael made a mental note to check the shift assignments. It'd be a shame to have Shayne—who was nearly a married man, after all—on duty during the shooting of this upcoming scene.

"I thought you were supposed to be the heroine. The good girl."

"I am. But my character goes undercover as a stripper to research a character in her book."

"And ends up dead in the bayou."

"You've read the script?"

"It seemed to be a wise precaution. Since the movie's already a play within a play, I figured your stalker could have decided to add another layer."

"Like an onion," she muttered.

"Exactly. Stalkers tend to be layered guys. They may be nuts, but there's a lot going on inside their heads. Sometimes you just have to be patient and peel away a layer at a time."

She could see him doing exactly that. He'd driven her crazy with his unyielding patience when they'd been teenage sweethearts. Obviously, his temperament, like forged steel, had only hardened over the years.

Although he'd insisted on keeping the drapes drawn and her internal clock was a little out of whack from her trip east, Lorelei sensed that it was getting late. The wind was kicking up; she could hear the fronds of the banana trees in the courtyard below beginning to scrape against the windows. Sulphurous flashes behind the closed draperies suggested lightning.

"A storm's blowing in from the Gulf," Michael said, as if reading her mind.

Now that she was aware of the weather, Lorelei realized that not all her nervousness was due to Michael's presence. She could practically taste the electricity in the artificially cooled air of the luxurious suite. Although she'd been born and bred in New Orleans, delta thunderstorms had always made her jumpy. Like Maggie in *Cat on a Hot Tin Roof.*

"That's all Eric needs. More delays."

"It should blow over by morning." His eyes gentled as he took in her renewed tenseness. "Remember that night the hurricane that had been forecast for Florida, hit here instead?"

"And we had to spend the night in your uncle's cabin." The memory, like so many others involving this man, was both good and bad. But mostly good. "I was scared to death."

"Me, too." He smiled reminiscently and leaned back in the chair, stretching out his long legs.

"You were frightened?" He'd hidden it so well,

calming her, drying her near hysterical tears, assuring her that he'd keep her safe. Which, of course, he had.

"That was one hell of a storm," he reminded her.

"Not as bad as the one that hit when we got home."

"I put you in danger taking you out there that weekend. Your dad had every right to want to knock my block off."

"Dad would never hit anyone. Violence is too undignified. Although I would have preferred an old-fashioned licking to being grounded for the rest of the summer."

"You and me, both, sweetheart."

Those had been the longest, most frustrating weeks of his life. They'd also been one of the few times when he'd purposefully gone against everything he'd been taught about truth and honor and discipline. There had been ways around Dr. Longstreet's edict. And for the rest of that long hot lonely summer Michael had done his utmost to discover every one.

"I wonder if that big oak is still beneath your window?"

She sighed. "It got root rot a few years ago. Mother wrote to tell me that they spent a fortune on tree surgeons trying to save it, but it was too far gone."

"Too bad." His warm smile hinted at intimate memories.

"I still can't believe you, of all people, did that—climbed into my bedroom all those nights."

"Hey, don't ever underestimate the power of teenage male hormones," he said with a quick grin. "The truth is, Lorelei, I was crazy about you. Enough to risk your father's wrath to be with you."

The conversation brought back, in vivid detail, all those long hot, silent petting sessions. Lorelei would never regret the things they'd done. There was also a part of her that wished Michael had been willing to carry their physical closeness to the inevitable conclusion.

"You told me I'd become an obsession," she reminded him.

They'd been lying on her bed, stuffed animals tossed to the floor. She'd been wearing the bottom of a pair of pink polka-dot baby doll pajamas. He'd been clad in a pair of faded jeans that contrasted with his bare chest, tanned to a deep mahogany by a summer spent working on the docks.

The sight, she recalled all too well, had made her dizzy then. The memory made her a little dizzy now.

"You had." *Obsession*. The word hovered in the thickening air. "I would have walked through the flames of hell to be with you back then, Lorelei, and welcomed the agony. Which is why I know—at least somewhat—what's going through your stalker's mind. You're all he càn think about...day or night.

"Which is why," Michael assured her, pushing himself out of the chair, "he'll slip up. His concentration's shot. He can't keep his distance much longer."

Lorelei stood up as well. "I'm not certain that's much of a comfort."

"It should be. Because as soon as he comes out of

the shadows, we'll get him." He took hold of both her upper arms. "And you can get on with your life."

At this moment, with his hands holding her, and his eyes warm and reassuring, Lorelei didn't really want to go anywhere. She was quite comfortable where she was, thank you. In fact, she wouldn't really mind if he were to draw her just the slightest bit closer....

She heard him murmur something and was certain the word must have come from her own fevered wishes.

"Excuse me? Did you say—"

"I said, 'Bed.'" Although he wasn't a man to reveal emotion, a flush rose from the collar of the navy polo shirt. "Your schedule shows an early shooting schedule. And you've already lost two hours coming from Pacific Coast time."

"You're right." She suddenly felt vastly tired. "Are you going to stay here?"

"I'll sleep on the couch."

"But I thought there were two bedrooms."

"With this living room between them. I'm willing to give you as much privacy as I can. But I'm going to have to stay close, too."

Like just on the other side of the door. The thought was far too appealing for comfort.

"Well, then. I guess I'll just go to bed."

"That's probably a good idea. I'll arrange a wake-up call. Do you want to run in the morning? Or if you'd rather use the gym on the roof, I can arrange for us to have it to ourselves."

She'd been away from home for a very long time.

Too long, Lorelei had realized as they'd driven to the French Quarter from the airport. She'd missed the city that was so unlike any other in America. More than she would have expected.

"If this storm blows over, I think I'd like to go running. If that's okay with you."

"Sure." His shrug drew her gaze to his broad shoulders again. And that pistol he hadn't taken off, reminding her that although they were getting along much better than she would have expected, this was not a social visit. "I run every morning. It'd be nice to have company."

That settled, Lorelei went into the adjoining bedroom, closing the door between them. She washed her face, brushed her teeth, then fell into the comfortable king-size bed. The stress of traveling, plus the unexpected appearance of Michael in her life had left her so exhausted that she was certain she'd fall asleep the moment her head hit the goose down pillows.

But instead, although her body was fatigued, her mind was wide awake. As she lay in the darkness, staring up at the ceiling, Lorelei found herself reliving, in Technicolor detail, every moment of their past life together.

Outside the heavily draped window, the wind kicked up, its lonely wail adding a counterpoint to the sounds of sirens in the Quarter. From the other side of the door, she heard a faint murmur of voices and decided that Michael must be watching television. One of those adult movies she'd seen advertised on the cardboard flyer atop the TV? she wondered. She rolled over and pounded her pillow with renewed force as the idea caused her nerve endings, which lately had only experienced fear, to spark and fire with something much more dangerous. And fiendishly hotter.

The cotton sheets were as smooth as silk. But when her overwrought mind imagined them to be Michael's wide rough hand, she rolled over again, onto her back. One of the pillows slid to the floor, but not before noisily knocking her water glass off the carved bedside table.

The door between them flew open. "What happened?"

"Nothing." The flickering glow from the television cast him in shadowed relief. He'd taken his shirt off, Lorelei noticed. And his feet were bare. When she noticed that he'd also unfastened the top button of his jeans, she felt like stuffing the sheet into her mouth to keep from moaning. "I just dropped my water glass."

She didn't know if he'd heard her. All his attention was on her body, clad in a peach satin nightshirt. Lorelei could feel it clinging to her aroused, hot damp skin and wondered if Michael could see her hardened nipples.

He could.

"Well, then." Michael dragged his eyes back to her face. "If you're sure you're all right."

She tried to answer, but the words had clogged in her throat. She swallowed and tried again. "Positive," she managed to reply.

"Okay." He dragged those long fingers she'd imagined creating havoc on her body through his jet hair, ruffling it in a way that made her want to press his head against her aching breasts. He looked at the pillow and top sheet that had ended up along with the glass on the floor. "Are you hot? I can adjust the air-conditioning."

"Really, Michael, I'm fine. I'm sorry to have bothered you."

His shoulders moved in a negligent shrug. "I was just watching TV. The news," he elaborated, in case she might think he'd been watching one of those dirty movies on her tab.

"Have they predicted the weather yet?"

"Showers through the night. Clearing by morning."

"That's good news. For Eric."

"Yeah. I guess so."

They stared at each other for another long minute.

"Good night, Lorelei." His voice was gruff.

"Good night, Michael." Hers was soft.

It took a Herculean effort, but Michael managed, just barely, to keep from slamming the door between them. He flung himself on the too short couch, his skin burning as if some maniac had put matches beneath it, and tried to concentrate as a very pregnant Desiree announced the birth of a new baby leopard at the Audubon Zoo.

The news anchor looked lovely, as always, although his practiced eye could see the faint purple shadows beneath her eyes that the heavy studio makeup could not quite cover up. She was obviously tired, which wasn't any surprise, considering her condition. Roman shouldn't let her work, Michael decided. Then laughed out loud at the thought of anyone—even Desiree Dupree Falconer's strong-willed husband—trying to tell her what to do.

Besides, he reminded himself, although they were still close friends, Desiree wasn't his business any longer. Which was just as well. Since the luscious female lying nearly naked in the bed just a few feet away on the other side of that door represented more of a problem than Michael had tackled during all his years on the force. He decided with grim humor that it'd be easier facing down a gangbanger with an Uzi in the projects than spend ten nights locked up in this hotel suite with America's sexy Ice Goddess.

Lorelei heard his deep rumbling laugh and hoped it wasn't directed at her. Whenever she'd fantasized about coming back to her home town, she'd thought about returning as a grand success, the type of glamorous, Hollywood star who ate men who dumped them—even if it was years ago—for breakfast.

She hadn't expected that flash of hormonal excitement she felt at the airport. Or worse, the return of the feeling she'd only ever experienced with him, a slow warmth that felt comforting and exciting all at the same time.

She didn't have time for this. She still had some of her most difficult scenes to film in a movie that was in serious trouble. She was being stalked by some crazed fan and although her parents were in Rome, they'd be returning before Lorelei left town, which meant that she'd probably end up in yet another argument about what they still considered her inappropriate career choice.

She didn't have time for an affair. She didn't have the emotional stamina to fall in love.

As she lay on her back in the too wide bed, listening to the sad and lonely patter of the rain against the window, Lorelei decided she was going crazy.

The rain, instead of cooling things down, only added to the humidity, and as she ran through the awakening streets of the French Quarter the following morning, Lorelei felt as if she were slogging through a wall of water. She was grateful to Michael for setting a reasonable pace; although she prided herself on staying in shape, she never could have kept up with his long muscular legs.

She allowed a stop at the Café du Monde, vowing to stick to coffee, but ended up devouring an order of beignets.

"If I keep this up, it's not going to be the good times rolling, but me," she moaned.

"Don't worry about it." Desire had claws as Michael watched her lick the snowy white sugar off her fingertips and forced down an urge to put those manicured pearl fingers into his own mouth. "It's a sacrilege to come to New Orleans and forgo the food."

"There's just too much temptation," she muttered, watching a tray of steaming hot cocoa pass by.

"You called that one right." Tossing his paper napkin on the table, Michael stood up. He would have preferred keeping her to himself all day long, but he wasn't being paid a thousand bucks a day—plus expenses—to fantasize about sprinkling powdered sugar all over her body, then licking it off. "We'd better get back. There's just time for a shower before you're due in makeup."

She could have sat there all day, watching the crowds, the little boy tap-dancing for change on the corner, the ornate white paddle boats cruising down the wide brown Mississippi along with all the other river traffic that had been the lifeblood of the delta for centuries.

But although some actors might be hedonists who caused difficulties and delays on a set, Lorelei was scrupulous about showing up on time, her lines memorized, ready to film. She stifled a sigh and left the bustling outdoor café.

DAMN HER! He'd thought Lorelei was different. He'd believed that she wasn't a slut, like all the other gorgeous women in Hollywood. Despite the outward packaging that practically screeched sin, he'd come to believe that deep down, where it really mattered, Lorelei Longstreet had a kind and sweet heart. In fact, there'd even been those occasions, when he'd watched the pale pink blush of roses bloom in her cheeks that he'd managed to convince himself she might even be a little shy.

He'd followed her this morning, watching her run in those baggy shorts that only made her slender legs appear even more enticing. One time, risking detection but unable to resist, he'd cut through Pirate's Alley, then stood in a doorway as she passed, close enough that if he'd wanted he could have reached out and touched those magnificent breasts that were bouncing so delightfully beneath that damp white oversize T-shirt.

The man, of course, would have stopped him. That huge beast that had been hovering over her like some overprotective police dog since she'd first arrived at the airport. He'd suspected, after the visit from the L.A. detective, that they might hire a bodyguard. He'd been expecting that, and although the unwelcome barrier annoyed him, he'd come to the conclusion that he could easily work around it. He was, after all, a clever man. A resourceful man. Everyone said so.

Except his mother. His brow furrowed as he thought about that harridan who'd made his life a living hell for so many years. Blood began to pulse in his temple, threatening to blow his head apart. That was the way his father had died. A stroke. Although she wasn't prosecuted, the man knew that his father's death had been murder. She'd killed him, pure and simple by making him lose his temper with her constant carping and criticizing.

And when her husband was buried, she'd turned her tormenting attention to her son, trying her best to destroy him.

But he'd proven stronger than his father. More daring. And now she was the one lying in the ground, dead and buried and good riddance to bad rubbish, that's what he always said.

The throbbing in his temple eased, the bloodred haze in front of his eyes cleared. His mind, far more agile than either of his loser parents—which had always made him suspect he'd been adopted—focused on the mission at hand.

In the beginning, he'd only wanted to love Lorelei. It bothered him that she didn't have a man in her life. He'd considered it a modern day tragedy that such a warmhearted, obviously sensual woman should have to lead a wasted, celibate existence.

But now, having seen her with the private detective, having seen the way they looked at each other, as if they were soppy, whiskey-drenched bread pudding the other just wanted to gobble up, he realized that he'd have to change the plan.

He'd watched them run together, like two thoroughbreds in harness, their legs hitting the uneven sidewalks of the Quarter in unison despite the difference in their sizes. He'd watched the ease with which they talked, the subtle little touch of his hand on her elbow, her fingers on the back of his wrist, when they foolishly, recklessly thought no one was looking.

They were too comfortable in each other's space, which could only mean one thing. They'd spent last night, locked away together in that penthouse suite of the Whitfield Palace, in bed together, sweating and groaning and tangling the sheets like some oversexed couple straight out of one of her movies. He wasn't going to blame the man. Everyone knew that males couldn't be responsible for their animalistic urges. If men weren't sexual beings, the world would have come grinding to a halt eons ago and human beings would have gone the way of the dinosaurs.

But even in this world of chaos, it was important to maintain some order. Some decorum. And that, of course, became the sacred role of women in society.

It was natural for every man who saw Lorelei to want her. Normal to fantasize about how that long pale hair would feel draped over his naked thighs, about how those glossy wet lips would feel swallowing his sex, about the soft, little cries she'd make when he hurt her, which he might have to do, for her own good, to teach her the proper way for a female to behave.

He'd believed her to be a goddess, but she'd betrayed him in the worst way possible, having sex with that oversize detective. And, perhaps even the man's brother, who'd been at the hotel with them for a time.

As a vision of a naked Lorelei twisting in the arms of both brothers at the same time—a virtual orgy of arms and legs and tongues—blazed in his tormented mind, the man made his decision.

He was going to have Lorelei. In all the ways he'd been fantasizing about for weeks. Then he was going to hurt her. And then, when he finally had the beautiful, treacherous slut begging for mercy, pleading for her worthless life, he was going to kill her.

# 6

WHILE THE DAY had lived up to the weather forecast, dawning bright and clear after the night rainfall, the sun was not shining in St. Louis Cemetery Number One, where Lorelei was scheduled to shoot her first New Orleans location scene.

Fog created by the special effects machines trailed along the ground, wrapping around her ankles like tentacles. The white tombs were draped in a thick gray haze.

"Spooky," she said, wrapping her arms around herself. Although the temperatures were already in the high eighties and climbing, the ghostly atmosphere made her feel strangely chilled.

"Glad you like it," a voice murmured from the mists. Lorelei started, then when she recognized Brian, her heart settled back down to a normal beat.

"Don't you ever write a scene that involves sunshine? And me staying dry?"

"What would be the point of that?" he asked with a grin. He turned his attention to Michael, who was standing silently beside Lorelei. "You must be O'Malley. The bodyguard."

"And you're Wilder. The writer."

"That's me." Brian cocked his head and gave Michael a closer, more professional perusal. "Eric mentioned the private detective business was a new enterprise for you."

Michael wondered if his credentials were being challenged. "Relatively new. But not so different from what I was doing."

"Oh, I wasn't suggesting you weren't good at your work," he assured Michael quickly. "I was just wondering if you'd considered any other occupation after leaving the police force."

"No."

Brian appeared undeterred by the brusque answer. "Perhaps I could convince you to consider acting."

"*Acting?*" The word exploded on a rough laugh. "Me? An actor?"

"You have a certain gritty quality that, if it could be captured on the screen would make you a perfect hero. Even bigger than Stallone or Schwarzenegger."

Michael wondered if everyone in Hollywood was so full of bullshit and decided, thinking back on his telephone conversations with Lorelei's director, they probably were. All except Lorelei, he amended. Somehow, it appeared she'd managed to stay incredibly well-grounded.

"Thanks anyway, but I think I'll just stick to what I'm doing," he said in a neutral tone.

"Well, sure. I can see where it'd be a real kick." Brian's gaze became teasingly seductive as it slid toward Lorelei. "Imagine guarding gorgeous women all day and night and actually getting paid for it."

"It has its rewards," Michael agreed dryly.

"I'll just bet." Brian rubbed his chin and gave the larger man another long look. "Well," he continued, "I can tell you're a man who likes to make up his own mind. But I'm working on a script that would be perfect for you, so if you decide you'd like to check out how you look on camera, just tell John that I told him to take a few shots."

Michael decided that camels and bedouins would be roaming the bayou before he took the writer up on that offer. "That'd be John Nelson."

"Yeah." Brian gestured with a thumb toward a tall blond man who was currently deep in conversation with the prop guy manning the fog machine. "John's one of those temperamental *artistes*, but nobody can capture a mood like he can." He made another swift examination of Michael's face. "He could make you look like you stepped off Mount Rushmore."

"Now there's a thought," Michael drawled to Lorelei as they crossed the set to where the director was going over the day's scenes outside the makeup trailer. Their shoes crunched on the crushed white shells that were used as gravel in this part of the country.

"He meant it as a compliment."

"I suppose so. But be truthful...can you see me doing this for a living?" It was as if they were all overgrown kids.

She shrugged and brushed at the tendril of mist that curled coldly on her cheek. "It's not that big a stretch."

"What?" He stopped in his tracks and stared down at her.

"You made your living playing cops and robbers,

for heaven's sake, Michael. Despite the seriousness of the crimes you must have had to deal with, being a policeman is not exactly a grown-up job."

He folded his arms. His only response was a grunt.

"And besides, I've watched enough television to guess that when you're in the Box—"

"Now there's a TV term if I ever heard one," he muttered.

"Taken from real life," she countered. "I know. I asked a real cop after I was signed to play a Los Angeles detective assigned to the vice squad."

"So you did some research." *Big deal*, he thought, but did not say.

She was not going to let him irritate her. Not before one of her more nerve-racking scenes. This would be the first time her fictional stalker actually touched her. And she was not looking forward to the prospect.

"The point is, when you were trying to get confessions out of the perps—" she scowled as she watched his gaze light up with wicked humor "—or suspects, or whatever you want to call them, isn't it true that the best actor usually wins?"

"I suppose it doesn't hurt to be able to play the role to your advantage," he allowed.

"See?" She tossed her hair back over her shoulder. "So you acted when you were a detective. And now you're a private detective, which is probably a secret fantasy of every little boy, right after cowboys and Superman. "

"I always wanted to be Batman. The costume's

cooler. A bat looks a helluva lot meaner than that big red *S*."

She smiled at that. "I rest my case. You're already acting, Michael. You have been for years. You just insist on calling it work."

She had a point, he decided reluctantly. "At least I get to call the shots." And hopefully, when he'd concluded a case there'd be one less bad guy on the streets.

"Point taken." It felt strange to be able to argue with Michael and not have it turn into some dangerous emotional battleground. Strange, but nice. "Are you going to stick around for the filming?"

"Sure."

"I wasn't certain. Since I won't be alone, I thought you might not worry about hanging around while I'm working."

"Taylor's paying for twenty-four hours. That's what he's going to get. Besides, money aside, we still don't know it's not someone on the crew, Lorelei. As long as you're in town, either Shayne or I will be right by your side."

"Even when I go to my parents' house for dinner?"

Just as Batman had the Riddler, Michael had always had the Longstreets. They hadn't approved of him when he'd been dating Lorelei. And he suspected nothing had happened in the intervening years to make her parents change their minds. But he was the boss of Blue Bayou Investigations. Which mean that the buck stopped on his scarred oak desk. There was no way he was going to send Shayne to face his nemeses.

"Are we invited to dinner?" he inquired with far more casualness than he was feeling.

"Not yet. But believe me, we will be." She smiled as she reached up and patted his grimly set cheek. "Don't worry, Michael. Perhaps I can have Dennis, from the prop department, round up a blindfold and cigarette for you."

With that she took off, walking through the mist toward Eric Taylor, who was deep in conversation with Wilder. The intense way the two of them were huddled together suggested they were planning an invasion, rather than merely making a movie. Michael leaned against a white marble pyramid-shaped tomb, folded his arms and watched as the cameraman, a tall blond man with obvious Scandinavian roots joined Lorelei.

"So," John Nelson said, casting a glance Michael's way, "that's the man Taylor hired to watch over you."

"That's him."

"He's certainly big enough."

"He is that," she agreed.

"And he looks strong."

"I'm sure he is."

"I suppose he carries a gun?"

"Unfortunately." She looked up at him. "Does that make you nervous, knowing an armed man is on the set?"

"On the contrary." The cameraman's pale blue eyes

glittered. "I think it's exciting." He paused. "I suppose he's quite the ladies' man."

"I wouldn't know." Lorelei didn't like thinking about Michael with other women. "Apparently he was involved with a local newscaster, but I guess that didn't work out."

"So he *is* heterosexual?"

"Of course." She suddenly realized the reason for his earlier question. "Oh, you didn't think—"

"Not me," John said quickly. A bit too quickly, Lorelei thought. "But Dennis thought there might be a chance." They both looked over at the man who had fog pouring out of the machine like clouds of steam from a teakettle. "He seemed quite taken with your macho bodyguard."

Lorelei would have had to have been deaf not to hear the note of aggravation—and jealousy—in the cinematographer's voice.

"Michael's a striking man. I can understand why anyone might be physically attracted to him." Now that, she considered, had to be the understatement of the millennium. Her hormones hadn't been the same since she stepped off that plane from Los Angeles. "But you and Dennis have been together for a long time, John—"

"We're celebrating our fifth anniversary next month."

"See?" She smiled reassuringly. "You don't have anything to worry about."

"Especially since your detective's not gay in the first place," John said robustly, as if needing to reassure himself. He looked at Michael again, taking in the un-wavering dark blue gaze directed their way. Then it was his turn to smile. "Looks as if you're the one who needs to worry, dear heart." That said, he joined the others to offer his professional take on the pivotal scene, and Lorelei turned toward the makeup trailer.

Her nerves were jangling as she sat in her chair in the trailer, having the waterproof foundation applied to her face with a damp sponge. She couldn't seem to help it. Perhaps it was the atmosphere generated by the tombstones and fog that was making her nervous.

"You realize," Michael, who was watching the transformation, said quietly, "you'd be nuts not to feel uneasy about this."

Frowning, she cast a quick warning glance up at the plump grandmotherly-looking woman.

"Don't worry about me," the woman said, smudging the dark kohl lining Lorelei's eyes with her thumb. "I never listen to conversations. Think of this chair as the confessional. It's totally private.

"Although," she added, as she drew a perfect scarlet line along the top of Lorelei's lips, "the detective's right. It'd only be natural for you to be scared to death, thinking about that sick son of a bitch out there watching you. Waiting."

Lorelei took the tissue square she was handed and blotted obediently. "Does everyone know about the stalker?" So much for maintaining some slim sense of privacy.

"Oh, sure." The liner was topped with two more coats of crimson color, then a slash of shiny gloss that would make Lorelei's lips appear perpetually wet. "But that's a good thing. Because this way we can all be watching out for anyone who doesn't belong on the set." She turned toward Michael. "Isn't that true?"

"I'm willing to take all the help I can get. And an extra, observant pair of eyes is always helpful." Lorelei noticed he failed to mention his belief that her stalker might be someone who belonged on the movie set.

"There, you see?" The woman smiled reassuringly as she brushed additional color along the crystal-sharp line of Lorelei's cheekbone. "We're all family, Lorelei, hon. You don't have to worry. We take care of our own." She hugged her with a genuine warmth that Lorelei had never experienced from her own mother. "You'll be just fine. And you look perfect. Doesn't she?" the makeup artist asked Michael.

"She's gorgeous," he agreed, his dark gaze backing his words. She looked, he thought, almost other-worldly.

"You are, you know," he said as they left the trailer together. "Absolutely gorgeous." He reached out, as if to skim a fingertip down her cheek, then pulled back, concerned he'd mar the carefully applied makeup. "You're also one of the gutsiest women I've ever met."

Lorelei found that remark more complimentary than his statement about her looks. "Why? Because I refuse to crumble when some sicko starts stalking me?"

"Some women would."

"Not me." She folded her arms and shook her head. "It wouldn't do any good and I refuse to give the creep the upper hand." She looked out over the cemetery, the white marble tombs making it appear to be a city of the dead, tamped down her fear and concentrated on her anger. "Besides, other women don't have the O'Malley brothers protecting them."

Although the topic was serious, his mood lightened. "Lucky you."

Her smile spread slowly. "That's exactly what I was thinking."

LORELEI WAS NOT SURPRISED when, ten minutes before filming, Brian handed her a sheaf of revisions.

"I don't understand," she said as she skimmed through the new pages. "I thought my character was being stalked by some guy she created in her mystery novel."

"She is," Brian agreed. "But when I saw Dennis working with the fog machine, inspiration struck and I decided it'd be cool to weave in a reincarnation subplot."

"About a lover from two hundred years in the past," she muttered as she continued to read. "So, now that we know she's making love to the guy at night in her dreams, are we supposed to believe that they've done some kind of mind meld that has her writing his biography during the day?"

Brian grinned. "Works for me."

"I do wish you could stick to the script for at least a day." She shot him a mock glare. "It's the computer age that's to blame. I'll bet you wouldn't be so eager to change things if you had to keep retyping the entire script."

He flashed another winning grin. "I replaced my old Selectric with a computer the day I sold my first script."

She shook her head in very real frustration. "I'm having trouble keeping my character's motivation intact with all these constant changes."

"Motivation's for those prima donna method actors. All you have to do is look intense and worried," the writer assured her. He gave her a quick kiss on the cheek, taking care not to smear her makeup, then left her to memorize the new pages, which, thankfully, contained very little dialogue.

Although she hadn't trained as a method actor, Lorelei always felt the need to understand the characters she played.

"All right," she said to herself, reviewing what she knew so far. "Mary Beth Wyndom has always considered herself an intelligent, highly logical person. Although she might create fiction for a living, her mystery plots are unrelentingly logical. A crime is committed. The intrepid heroine detective, following an orderly series of clues, inevitably closes her case by hard work, deductive reasoning, and dogged determination."

That's the character she'd been playing up until now. A character who seemed to have made the decision to allow other writers to dwell on the fanciful— on vampires and ghosts and things that went bump in the night.

"She's never accepted the idea of voodoo, or wishes." Indeed, from what Lorelei had inferred from the scenes of the woman at home, her parents, professors of law at Tulane University, had not encouraged her to believe in the Tooth Fairy, the Easter Bunny, or Santa Claus.

"If they knew I've fallen in love with a man from the past, if they suspected I'm meeting that man at his own tomb two centuries after his death, they'd have me committed. For my own good, of course."

Watching her, listening to her use of the first person pronoun, Michael suspected Lorelei didn't even realize she'd slipped into her character's skin. He decided she could have been in another world. Which she was...

He was only a figment of her imagination, she'd told herself each night. He wasn't real.

But, dear heavens, her need—no, that wasn't strong enough—her *hunger* was all too real. And so, it seemed, was his.

Every morning, the bruises and bite marks on her flesh were proof that although she hadn't left the room, had opened the door to no one, she'd been thoroughly ravished. The passion—and the marks—had escalated with each passing night. But incredibly, they'd only left her wanting more....

"Show time, Lorelei," a voice called out, shattering her sensual thoughts.

Lorelei blinked, looked around and saw Michael standing a few feet away, arms crossed, looking at her with grave interest.

"That was fascinating."

"What?" Her mind was splintered; she couldn't understand his words.

"Watching your mind work. Do you always become your characters?"

"Not always." She blinked again as reality began to sink in. "But Brian's good. His constant rewriting is a pain, but he always creates characters I can identify with." She smiled a little self-consciously. "Sometimes it's almost as if we're in each other's heads."

As she walked to her mark, stopping to speak briefly with Wilder, Michael found himself hating the idea of Lorelei having any kind of damn mental telepathy with the hotshot Hollywood writer.

When the cameras began rolling, Lorelei became Mary Beth Wyndom. She knew Mary Beth's thoughts. Hopes. And fears.

The crew, the cameras, the fog machine, the microphone over her head, *everything* from her everyday working world, all faded from her consciousness.

She was now all alone in the cemetery. The tombs, barely visible through the thick swirling fog, stood silent, like mute white ghosts. She was wearing a gauzy lavender dress that seemed created from the very mist that curled in clinging tendrils around her bare arms and calves. In the stuttering, veiled early morning light her skin looked as smooth, and felt as cold, as the marble surrounding her. A sprig of white flowers was pinned above her breast.

As she made her tentative way across the uneven, shell-strewn ground, she briefly wondered what insane impulse had her wearing such impractical, spindly high heels. Such vanity could be dangerous. That thought made her laugh, the silvery sound echoing in the fog. As if her entire reason for coming here today wasn't already fraught with danger.

The smell of impending rain rode the air scented with camellias, jasmine, magnolias and diesel oil from the nearby river. She tripped over an urn of plastic flowers and stumbled to her knees, catching hold of a corner of a tomb that was sinking into the marshy ground.

As she clung to the cold damp stone, she thought she heard someone whisper her name...Mary Beth...but decided it was only the sound of the leaves brushing together overhead.

Pulling herself up to her feet, she continued on, weaving her way through the tombs, stopping now and then when she thought she heard the soft sounds of gravel crunching behind her. But whenever she'd pause, all she could hear were the muffled sounds of Basin Street traffic and the high, sad sweet song of an alto sax from somewhere in the French Quarter.

Her nerves were jangling, her pulse hammered in her throat. She swallowed and tasted the metallic flavor of fear. And the sweeter, honeyed taste of anticipation.

She could feel him. Watching her. Waiting. And amazingly, although it didn't make any sense, although every logical bone in her body told her that it was impossible, she knew that the man she had come here to meet, the man who'd been haunting her dreams, knowing her every need, understanding how she liked to be kissed, touching her exactly where she longed to be touched, was the same man she'd based her current novel on.

A man who'd been dead for two hundred years.

She passed a tomb covered with brick dust *x*'s. Coins, shells and beads littered the ground around it. The tomb allegedly belonged to Marie Laveau, the nineteenth-century voodoo queen. The *x*'s signified wishes, the offerings left in appreciation for wishes granted, or "just in case."

She'd finally reached her destination. The hammering in her throat calmed even as her blood warmed in anticipation.

"I've come, Philippe." She ran her fingertips over the name carved into the gleaming white stone. Philippe Villars Marigny de Dubreuil, reckless, dashing, youngest son of a wealthy Creole planter who'd been killed in a duel. Some of his detractors had called Philippe a pirate. Others a devil.

But to her, he was everything.

"Mary Beth." Her name whispered over her face, touched her eyes, which fluttered obediently closed, teased at her lips, which could already taste his Virginia grown tobacco and French brandy. "*Ma Belle.*"

Mary Beth had known, when he'd first appeared in her bedroom, with his clever hands and wicked lips, that as magical as it was, their togetherness had the impermanence of the insubstantial fog that wrapped around them whenever they made love. In the beginning, she'd told herself that it was enough, that since no man had ever loved her with such passion, since no other man had ever made her feel so alive, so much of a woman, she was willing to accept this temporary coming together.

But it was no longer enough. Having prepared for this night, she'd made numerous visits to the Voodoo Museum on St. Ann, purchased gris-gris at the adjoining gift shop, burned incense and left coins for Marie Laveau and even journeyed out into the bayou to meet with a self-proclaimed voodoo priestess.

And now, finally, she was ready.

Her fingers began unfastening the pearl buttons between her breasts. One by one they gave way and when the dress was finally open to the hem, she shrugged, allowing it to fall off her shoulders, where it drifted to the gleaming white gravel like a filmy lavender cloud. Beneath the dress she was wearing a virginal white lace teddy that shimmered like moonlight, and white lace-topped stockings that ended high on her thighs.

"I've come, Philippe," she whispered. She closed her eyes again and extended her arms in a mute sensual invitation.

She did not have long to wait. When she felt the strong fingers curl around her neck, she tilted her head back, offering the paleness of her throat. Her hair fell down her back like a pale waterfall, her lips parted expectantly.

"So you have, my dear." The fingers, encased in black leather, tightened. As her eyes flew open in shock, Mary Beth found herself staring not into the loving dark eyes of her phantom dream lover, but at a demon born of her worst nightmares.

She opened her mouth to scream, but those dark treacherous fingers cut off all sound. She saw the glint of a scalpel, felt the cold slice of steel against her suddenly icy flesh.

Then everything went dark....

A long silence settled over the cemetery. Eric Taylor finally broke it.

"Cut," he called out, his voice lacking its usual assertion.

"Cut," the assistant director echoed, his own voice shakier than usual.

"Christ," Brian Wilder murmured.

"Got it in one," John Nelson said with pleasure.

Michael looked down at the scantily dressed Lorelei lying seemingly lifeless on the gravel, wrapped in artificially produced fog, and couldn't say anything.

# 7

FORTY-FIVE MINUTES LATER Lorelei was sitting with the crew in a booth at the Acme Oyster House. Befitting the laid-back Big Easy atmosphere, a nearby sign announced that a waitress was available—sometimes.

Even with her face scrubbed free of the heavy theatrical makeup and clad in jeans and a T-shirt, she'd garnered more than a little attention. Watching the patrons of the popular New Orleans establishment eyeing her with interest, Michael realized that Lorelei would probably never be free to live a truly private life.

"That strangled scream was a nice touch, Lorelei," Brian said. He tossed back an oyster and followed it up with a swallow of draft beer.

"Made the scene," Eric agreed, polishing off his vodka gimlet and catching the waitress's eye for another.

"I wasn't exactly acting at the time." The memory frightened her. Lorelei took a sip of iced tea and willed her mind back to something resembling calm. "Why didn't you tell me that you'd written that scalpel into the scene?"

Brian shrugged. "Since Eric and I decided to toss it

in at the last minute, we thought it might get more of a reaction if you didn't know about it ahead of time."

"It worked great, Lorelei," John assured her with the enthusiasm of a man who loved his work. "Wait until you see the dailies. I was using a handheld camera that'll give it a shaky, psychological edge."

"I thought, for a moment, that the scalpel was real," she complained. She stabbed a piece of romaine. Although she was attempting to be good and stick to her salad, she'd already slipped and allowed herself two of the restaurant's specialties. How fattening could oysters on the half shell be?

"Did it ever occur to you creative geniuses that Michael might have thought so, as well? Someone could have gotten shot."

"Of course we thought of that, darling," Eric assured her. "Which is why we informed Mr. O'Malley of the change."

She shot him a look. "You knew I was going to get scared to death?"

He shrugged, chewed the bite of fried catfish he'd just put in his mouth and wondered how the hell he'd gotten dragged into the movie business.

"I knew the script had been changed," he said after he'd swallowed. "I didn't realize how strong the new scene was going to turn out to be."

"Well." She shook her head as she studied the four men she'd thought she could trust. "You all probably would be feeling a lot less pleased with yourselves if I'd dropped dead of a heart attack right on the spot."

"Couldn't happen," Brian assured her with his

trademark cocky grin. "You've got the heart of a trooper, Lorelei. Hitchcock's probably kicking in his grave, frustrated that he missed the chance to work with you."

She refused to allow such blatant flattery to diminish her lingering pique. "Speaking of graves, am I at least allowed to ask if the man stalking me—the two-hundred-year-old dead man—is also a vampire?"

"I haven't decided that yet," Brian admitted. "It'd make a nice touch...."

"Especially if you decide to join him on the dark side," Eric said.

"And blood is always so challenging to film," John added cheerfully.

"But it may just turn out that you're nuts and imagining everything that's happening to you," Brian said.

"You guys are nuts," she muttered.

"That goes without saying." Brian reached over and ruffled her hair in a friendly, fraternal gesture. "And, for the record, so are you darlin'. If we weren't, we'd all be working for IBM. Or selling insurance."

On that depressing note, the conversation drifted off and everyone returned their attention to lunch.

Shayne, looking outrageously dapper in black jeans, a black silk T-shirt and a cream raw silk jacket that Lorelei immediately recognized as an Armani, arrived during the argument over what to order for dessert.

"Someone call for a private detective?" he asked cheerfully.

"My God," John Nelson murmured in Lorelei's ear. "Who is that Greek god?"

"Shayne O'Malley," she murmured back. "The youngest brother."

"Youngest?" The cameraman's blond brow climbed his forehead as he looked from Shayne to Michael, then back again. "There are more than two?"

"Three. Roarke's the middle one."

"Does he look—"

"As good as the others."

"It's just a good thing we got the fog scene out of the way. Because I doubt if we'll get another decent bit of work out of Dennis all day long," John predicted with a long-suffering sigh.

As she watched Michael introduce his brother to the other men at the table, and noted the relaxed masculinity Shayne exuded, Lorelei decided the cameraman might just be right.

The afternoon filming went faster. Since it was mostly shots of scenery, designed to set mood and place, Lorelei strolled along the levee, checked out the artists outside the gates of Jackson Square and rode the ferry—the one Sandra Bullock had made famous in *The Pelican Brief*—across the river to Algiers Point, then back again.

And although she knew Shayne was nearby the entire time, his steady presence didn't cause the same simmering sexual awareness she'd felt when his brother watched her.

By late afternoon, long blue shadows were drifting over the Quarter, causing John to announce he was losing the light.

"It's just as well," Eric decided. "Might as well

knock off early so those of us who promised their kids souvenirs can get some shopping done before that reception tonight."

Damn. The reception had completely slipped her mind. After the day she'd put in, Lorelei had been looking forward to a long soak in the tub, room service, and perhaps a comedy on the movie channel. Unless, of course, Brian gave her another blizzard of changes to memorize.

"Eric—"

"No way, kiddo." Guessing what she was about to ask, he put up a hand, forestalling her argument. "The city has cooperated with us every step of the way on this film, even paying for off duty cops to keep the crowds away. In return for this largesse, the mayor, along with several other influential local citizens, wishes to get his picture taken with America's sex goddess. I, for one, am not going to deny him the opportunity."

Even though she knew he had a point, Lorelei was still not looking forward to an evening spent in high heels making small talk with politicians.

"There are times when I wish we were back in the old days," she muttered. "When movies were all made on sets in gigantic sound stages and we didn't have to kiss up to every mayor, police commissioner and city council member whenever we wanted to film on location."

"Schmoozing is part of the business," he said with the ease of a man who did such socializing often and easily. "And don't forget, sweetheart, back in those so-called good old days, you'd be expected to audition on your back on a casting couch."

"There is that," she acknowledged crossly. She tried another tack. "I forgot to bring anything appropriate for a reception."

"No problem. You can borrow something from wardrobe."

"Let's see, that leaves me with a choice of a dress covered with fake blood, a see-through teddy, or those pasties and G-string I'm still getting up nerve to wear for the stripper scene."

"Go shopping. We'll write it off as promo expense."

"You're expecting me to find a suitable outfit just like that?" She snapped her fingers.

"Why not? If my wife can spend the equivalent of the treasuries of the entire Third World in a single afternoon on Rodeo Drive, you should be able to find a simple cocktail dress."

Surrendering to the inevitable, Lorelei caved in, as she'd known from the beginning she would.

"So," she asked Shayne with studied casualness as they headed toward the shopping district on Canal Street, "did Eric rope you into accompanying me to the mayor's reception?"

"Actually, that's Michael's gig. He takes the nights and mornings," he explained. "I pick up the middle of the day."

"I see." She thought about that. "I suppose I'm not your only case."

"No." He grinned down at her. "Just our most important."

Lorelei smiled back. She could almost forget the reason for Shayne's presence, almost pretend they were simply friends taking a late afternoon stroll through the Quarter.

"I still can't believe you've settled down," she said as they passed the Old Absinthe House, where Andrew Jackson and the Lafitte brothers had supposedly plotted the defense of the city back in 1815. At some time since then the custom had begun of putting calling cards on the wall; the browning cards resembled layers of peeling wallpaper. "You always insisted New Orleans was too small for you."

"I had a lot of plans," he agreed. "Lived a lot of them, too."

"As a spy?" She'd heard the remarkable rumor from a cousin who'd run into Shayne O'Malley in the mountains of Tibet several years ago.

"A government agent," he corrected mildly. "Sort of a traveling bureaucrat."

There was no way she could envision this man as a mere bureaucrat, but deciding there was no point in arguing, she shifted the topic to what she really wanted to know.

"Michael also mentioned something about you being serious about a woman?" Her cousin Savannah had waxed nostalgic about her hot, short-lived affair with the sexy O'Malley brother.

"Her name is Bliss." Just the way his voice warmed, drawing the name out, lingering over it, told Lorelei that whoever she was, the woman likely had a great deal to do with Shayne's deciding to put down roots.

"Bliss Fortune. She owns an antique shop—The Treasure Trove. She's also technically my landlady since The Blue Bayou offices are upstairs."

"You never did mention why Michael caught you breaking into those offices," Lorelei mused.

"It's a long story, but the condensed version is that I thought Bliss was an international jewel thief and I was trying to get the goods on her. At the time, I had no idea Michael had rented the offices upstairs. Hell, I was as surprised to see him as he was to see me."

So that's how they came to be holding guns on each other. The chilling thought made her shiver.

"It all turned out okay," Shayne assured her. His pale blue eyes, like Michael's dark ones, appeared not to miss a thing. "Neither of us got shot, Bliss turned out to be innocent—just like Michael had insisted all along, which she'll never let me forget—and if she wasn't so damn stubborn, we could just live happily ever after."

Lorelei couldn't resist a faint smile at his suddenly aggrieved tone. "Don't tell me there's a woman in this world capable of resisting your masculine charms?"

She knew Shayne was truly upset when her dry tone flew right over his head. "She didn't exactly turn me down. Well, she did make me crawl, but after the way I'd lied to her about who, and what, I was, I understood that. It's the timing that's got me so damn frustrated."

He stopped and looked down at her, his handsome face more miserable than she ever remembered seeing it. Even back when his famous father, who'd been taking his award-winning news photographs throughout the Middle East, had failed to show up for his ninth birthday party.

"Do you have time for a drink? I need a woman's advice on something."

She didn't bother to glance down at her watch. Shayne had always been a good friend. If he needed to talk, she'd be willing to risk Michael's irritation, and being late for the mayoral bash, which in truth, wasn't any real sacrifice.

"I'd better stick to tea since it could be a long night," she said. "And I've got another early call in the morning. But I'd love a chance to talk without an audience."

Without Michael. The all-important name went unspoken, but both knew they were thinking it.

They stopped at a little local bar where the sawdust on the floor was fresh, the glasses were clean and the jazz was cool.

Shayne waited until the drinks—iced tea sprigged with mint for her, beer for him—were served, along with a basket of spicy popcorn shrimp that Lorelei knew she should ignore. But, of course, didn't.

"I've bought a house," he revealed.

"Congratulations."

"It's not real big, but it's got enough room for kids. And Bliss has a real eye for turning bare rooms into a home."

"So you're living together?"

"Yeah. For the past couple of months." He scowled and traced a finger down the dew on the outside of his pilsner glass. "But we're not just shacking up or anything. I mean, I've proposed to her. And she accepted."

"Even better." Lorelei smiled and wondered what the problem was.

"The thing is, she's pregnant."

"Oh." From his mention of kids, she'd assumed he and Bliss wanted children. "So the timing's wrong?" she ventured carefully.

"Exactly!" He hit his fist on the pine table, causing a few shrimp to jump out of the basket. "I want to get married right away, you know, make an honest woman of her."

Lorelei had to reign in her smile at that old-fashioned expression. It was obvious that Michael wasn't the only chauvinistic O'Malley brother. "But she wants to wait?"

"That's what she says," he grumbled.

"Perhaps," Lorelei suggested, "she's afraid you're only marrying her because of the baby—"

"I told you, I'd already proposed. And she accepted."

"That's right." Beginning to be as confused as he looked, she popped a couple of fried shrimp in her mouth and chewed thoughtfully. "Perhaps she doesn't want to be a pregnant bride. Most women fantasize about their weddings from the time they're little girls. Maybe she doesn't want to feel fat when she walks down the aisle."

"She's not even showing yet," Shayne countered. "Except her breasts, which are really getting magnificent...but I guess you don't need to hear that part...."

He sighed and dragged a frustrated hand through his hair in a gesture that reminded her of Michael.

"If we got married right now, like I want to, she could wear whatever damn dress she wanted and no one would ever know. And it's not exactly like people count months anymore. And anyone who does isn't really a friend anyway, right?"

"Right." She leaned back, took another sip of tea and eyed him over the rim of the heavy glass. "I'm afraid I don't understand. Have you told her how you feel? Or explained why you want to marry her now?"

"Of course."

"And?"

"And she says that there's no way she's going to marry me before Labor Day."

"That's not too far off."

"It is for me. Besides, it's Bliss's cockeyed reasoning I can't agree with."

"You've lost me again."

"She insists she doesn't want to steal the thunder from Roarke and Daria."

"Roarke's getting married?"

"Yeah, on Labor Day. To Daria Shea, a local prosecutor. He quit the network a few months ago and now they're living in her house in the Irish Channel while he writes a book about his adventures as a hotshot network war correspondent."

Amazing. It seemed that two of the three O'Malley brothers had been struck with a sudden case of domesticity. She wondered if there was something in the air. Or perhaps the water.

"So," Shayne said, returning the conversation to its original track, "what do you think I should do?"

"I suppose allowing Bliss to make her own decision is out of the question?"

"She's pregnant," he reminded her. "Her hormones are swinging all over the place right now. It's obvious that she can't make an informed decision."

Personally, Lorelei doubted that, but not knowing Bliss, and not wanting to annoy the man she was going to be spending a great deal of time with over the next week, she tried for a middle ground.

"I guess," she said slowly, carefully, "you're just going to have to convince her to see things your way."

"Yeah." Shayne grinned. "That's just what I was thinking." He leaned over and kissed her cheek. "Thanks, Lorelei. You're a peach."

He was admittedly chauvinistic. Probably, she concluded, even somewhat dictatorial. But sweet. As she returned the irresistible smile, Lorelei assured herself that any woman intrepid enough to agree to marry any of the O'Malley brothers would undoubtedly be able to handle a little pressure.

Or in this case, she considered, viewing the blue flame in his determined eyes, a lot.

SHE LOOKED touched by magic. Michael stood up as Lorelei emerged from the bedroom of the hotel suite and tried not to drool.

The dress—if you could call such a strapless slither of beaded silk a dress—slicked down her body like rainfall. It was silver, almost as pale as her hair and

# NO COST! NO OBLIGATION TO BUY!
# NO PURCHASE NECESSARY!

## PLAY "LUCKY 7" AND GET FIVE FREE GIFTS

# HOW TO PLAY:

1. With a coin, carefully scratch off the silver box at the right. Then check the claim chart to see what we have for you—FREE BOOKS and a gift—ALL YOURS! ALL FREE!

2. Send back this card and you'll receive brand-new Harlequin Temptation® novels. These books have a cover price of $3.50 each, but they are yours to keep absolutely free.

3. There's no catch. You're under no obligation to buy anything. We charge nothing—ZERO—for your first shipment. And you don't have to make any minimum number of purchases—not even one!

4. The fact is thousands of readers enjoy receiving books by mail from the Harlequin Reader Service®. They like the convenience of home delivery...they like getting the best new novels BEFORE they're available in stores...and they love our discount prices!

5. We hope that after receiving your free books you'll want to remain a subscriber. But the choice is yours—to continue or cancel, anytime at all! So why not take us up on our invitation, with no risk of any kind. You'll be glad you did!

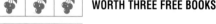

# THE HARLEQUIN READER SERVICE®: HERE'S HOW IT WORKS

Accepting free books places you under no obligation to buy anything. You may keep the books and gift and return the shipping statement marked "cancel". If you do not cancel, about a month later we'll send you 4 additional novels, and bill you just $2.90 each plus 25¢ delivery per book and applicable sales tax, if any.* That's the complete price—and compared to cover prices of $3.50 each—quite a bargain! You may cancel at any time, but if you choose to continue, every month we'll send you 4 more books, which you may either purchase at the discount price…or return to us and cancel your subscription.

*Terms and prices subject to change without notice. Sales tax applicable in N.Y.

studded with glittering, starlike crystals. Rather than
the expected diamonds, rhinestones sparkled brightly
at her ears, falling almost to bare alabaster shoulders.

"Well," he said around a tongue that felt abnor-
mally thick and heavy, "if you wanted to draw your
stalker out of hiding, I couldn't think of more effective
bait."

"I don't want to think about him tonight." Thinking
Michael looked wonderful in his navy suit, crisp white
shirt and flag red tie, she held out a bracelet. "And I'm
not going to slink around in sackcloth and ashes just
because he might be out there somewhere."

"He's out there, all right." He frowned as he fastened the now familiar diamond bracelet on the wrist
she'd extended toward him. The faintly regal gesture
reminded him of a princess summoning her footman.

Michael's gritty tone was at odds with the flash of
masculine appreciation she'd seen in his eyes when
she'd entered the room. Although she wasn't about to
admit it, when she'd talked Shayne into stopping at
the Canal Street Maison Blanche department store for
something appropriate to wear tonight, Lorelei hadn't
gone shopping with the mayor in mind.

"You sound very sure of that."

"I am." The scent of white roses surrounded his
head like a fragrant cloud, making Michael wish that
they were just two people about to enjoy an evening
on the town, rather than a private detective and a client he was trying to keep alive. "The guy called while
you were out with Shayne buying up the French
Quarter."

"Called?" She glanced over at the ivory telephone. "Here?" The idea had never occurred to her. She realized that she'd had such faith in Michael's ability to protect her she'd never considered the possibility her stalker might try to contact her while he was on duty.

"He left a message on your hotel voice mail. It was waiting when I got here this evening."

"I never even thought to check it." She dragged a distracted hand through her hair. "What time did he call?"

Not that it mattered, she thought. But she needed to know. Needed to think back on what she'd been doing while he'd been trying to terrify her.

"The recorder had it down as 5:05."

At five o'clock she'd been standing in her bra and panties in the department store dressing room, trying on dress after dress, determined to find one that would knock the unflappable Michael O'Malley's socks off.

"Did you recognize his voice?"

"It was impossible. He was running it through an electronic device that distorted it."

"And made it sound like someone from the *Star Wars* bar scene."

"Yeah. You've heard it before."

"Unfortunately." She breathed deeply, determined to remain calm. "What did he say?"

Michael shrugged and looked uncomfortable. "The usual. It was just sick garbage, Lorelei. You don't need to hear that stuff."

No, she decided, she didn't. Especially since she remembered all too well the droning, strangely mechanical voice murmuring about all the horrible things her unseen stalker intended to do to her. Everything he was going to force her to do to him. Michael was right. The man, whoever he was, was very, very sick.

"Was it...could you tell...did he call long distance?" She hated the tremor she heard in her voice. Hated the way just the thought of her stalker could turn her knees to water.

"It was a local call." He studied her as if trying to make a decision. "It was obvious he'd been watching you." Another pause. "He mentioned Shayne showing up at the Oyster House... And the scene you filmed in the cemetery. Including the scalpel that wasn't in the earlier version of any script."

"What?" A bubble of panic broke through her forced calm. Her blood drained from her carefully made up face, chilling her skin to ice as she lowered herself shakily into the nearest chair. "He was there?"

No wonder she'd felt as if the scene were all too real. At the time she'd dismissed her nervousness as stress from Brian having changed the spooky scene at the last minute. Now she realized she'd sensed him. Watching. Waiting.

"Oh, God." She covered her face with her hands and began to tremble.

"Hey, it's okay." Michael's reaction was instantaneous. One moment he was standing beside the antique desk, watching her carefully, the next he was gathering her into his arms. One wide capable hand stroked her hair. "In a way, this is good."

She rested her forehead against the solid line of his shoulder, remembering how, when he'd worked on the docks, he'd been able to lift more cargo than much larger and older men. Although she realized that strength had more to do with character than muscles and straining biceps, she also knew that Michael had plenty of both. And while she had her own share of inner strength, Lorelei was willing to let him shoulder this burden. For now.

"I don't want to argue with you, Michael," she said on a hitch of breath against his suit jacket. "But it's obvious that we have a vastly different definition of *good*."

"He slipped up." He took her chin between his fingers and tilted her fretful gaze up to his reassuring one. "The off duty police the mayor provided had the cemetery blocked off for the filming," he reminded her.

Curiosity overcame fear. "So?"

"So, there was no way for any civilian to get close enough to see what was happening."

"He could have used binoculars," she mused. "Or a telephoto lens. I made a movie last year about a woman photographer who became obsessed with this policeman and began stalking him—"

"*Dangerous Passions*," he said. "I saw that one." Along with half the population. "You were great, by the way."

"Thank you," she said softly, liking the idea of him caring enough to go to her film, wondering if he'd sat in the dark and thought about her. Thought about what might have happened if things had been different. If he hadn't dumped her all those many years ago.

The idea nearly made her laugh out loud. Here she was, being stalked by a madman and she was still obsessed by a teenage love affair.

"What's the matter?"

She'd begun trembling again. Her eyes glistened with unshed moisture. He'd faced innumerable dangers during his years working New Orleans's mean streets, including a couple of bullets he hadn't managed to dodge. But Michael wasn't certain he'd be able to handle this woman's tears.

"Nothing." She sniffled. Blinked. Then, to his amazement, a soft shaky giggle escaped those full lips he'd been dying to taste. "As ridiculous as it sounds under the circumstances, I was just hoping you'd suffered while you were watching my movie."

"Like the damned." His tone was gruff, but reluctant humor sparked in his gaze. "Does that make you feel better?"

"Actually, I think it does."

"Then I suppose it was worth it."

They'd have to talk about it, he realized. What had happened between them. And why. And what, if anything, remained after all these years. But this was neither the time nor the place. There'd be plenty of opportunity for discussion after he'd caught her stalker. Michael refused to accept the possibility that he might fail.

"As good as that movie was, your stalker couldn't have used the same technique," he said. "It would have been impossible to see through all that damn fog the prop guy was cooking up."

"Dennis," she murmured nonsensically. "His name is Dennis."

"Yeah. Nelson's significant other. Which should put him out of the running, too."

There was something in his voice. Something hard and frightening. "But it doesn't?"

"I'm not ruling anyone out, Lorelei. At first, the guy could have been any weirdo in Los Angeles." His tone suggested that in his opinion, that included most of the population of her adopted city. "But now, thanks to that phone call, we've at least narrowed the list of suspects down to a workable number."

That idea, which should have given her some scant comfort, didn't. Because if Michael was right, then the man who'd been terrifying her was at the very least an acquaintance. And worse yet, perhaps even someone she considered a friend.

"It'll be okay," he assured her yet again.

And because it was Michael telling her so, Lorelei believed him.

# 8

THE MAYOR'S RECEPTION was held in a banquet room at
the Jean Lafitte Hotel in the French Quarter. It seemed
as if everyone who was anyone in Louisiana had been
invited. Lorelei found herself being introduced to a
seemingly nonending parade of politicians, society
mavens, several professional football players and two
faces she recognized immediately.

Since Roman Falconer was one of her favorite writers—and a former neighbor—she would have enjoyed
seeing him on any occasion. But, in truth, at the moment she was more interested in his wife, local television anchor Desiree Dupree Falconer.

"What a pleasant surprise," she said, smiling up at
the novelist. "I bought your new book at LAX, but
never expected to run into you while I was in town."

"The Queen of the Vampires is away on a book
tour," Roman said with a quick grin that was a striking contrast to his dark, severely chiseled features. "I
was the best the mayor could round up at the last minute."

"I don't believe that. Your books are riveting. Especially the two with the serial rapist and killer. The se-
quel gave me nightmares for weeks."

"Me, too," he said simply, although the quick look

he exchanged with his wife suggested something he wasn't prepared to share.

"I watched your newscast while I was getting ready tonight," Lorelei said, turning to Desiree. "You're very good."

"Thank you." Desiree's smile was unforced, but vaguely distant. Lorelei felt herself being measured by this woman who'd once been intimately involved with Michael. A woman whose bright hair and gleaming amber eyes made Lorelei feel pale and washed out. "I've always admired your work, as well."

Before Lorelei could reply, Desiree looked up at Michael. "Hi." This time her smile was echoed in her eyes.

"Hi, yourself, gorgeous." He gave her a hug that Lorelei decided lasted way too long.

Watching him take the beautiful woman into his arms, she felt a sudden stab of jealousy, never mind that the woman in question was visibly pregnant beneath a dark bronze silk dress that matched her hair. Apparently, Roman suffered no such misgivings. From what Lorelei could tell, he was remarkably at ease with the obvious friendship his wife shared with her former lover.

A silence settled over the two couples as Desiree gave Lorelei another of those quiet, assessing looks.

"You know," Roman said, rocking back on his heels, "it's hard to believe that the little girl who used to ride her bike across my parents' lawn grew up to be a movie star."

Since she'd begun to feel ridiculously nervous, and

too much like high school for comfort, Lorelei could
have kissed him for breaking the lingering quiet.

"You would have to remember that."

He chuckled. "Those tire tracks used to drive the
gardener nuts." He glanced back and forth between
his wife and Lorelei. "Talk about your small worlds. If
your grandmother hadn't sent you off to boarding
school after your parents died," he said to Desiree,
"you and Lorelei would have been in the same class."

"Isn't that a coincidence," she murmured, glancing
again at Michael.

Another little silence drifted over the foursome.

"So," Roman said, trying again to dispel the building tension, "how long are you going to be home?"

"So long as the weather continues to cooperate,
we'll be here another week."

"That long," Desiree murmured.

"Yes." Lorelei met her gaze with a level, faintly
challenging look of her own. "That long."

She was surprised when Desiree's expression suddenly warmed, as if Lorelei had gained her approval.
And then she thought she understood why the
woman had been so cool and distant. She was Michael's friend and she'd been measuring Lorelei as she
might any woman who had come with him. Desiree
didn't know Michael was accompanying her because
he was paid to and Lorelei decided she certainly
wasn't going to tell her.

"I realize you're going to be incredibly busy," Desiree said. "But perhaps, while you're in town, we can

get together for dinner." Her gaze swept over to include Michael. "The four of us."

"Sounds great," Michael agreed before Lorelei—who'd been about to claim a horrendous shooting schedule—could refuse.

"It's a date, then." Roman glanced over at the mayor, who was shifting from foot to foot and looking impatient. "Oh-oh. Looks as if we're keeping you from your fans."

Lorelei followed his gaze and had to stifle her groan. "That's not a fan," she said flatly. "That's my mother."

Knowing that she had no choice, Lorelei started weaving her way through the rich and locally famous crowd. "Please," she murmured, "don't tell my mother you're being paid to guard me."

"I wouldn't think of it." Although he'd never thought of himself as the kind of man to hold a grudge, Michael rather enjoyed the idea of pretending to be Lorelei's date for the evening. Especially after all Maureen Longstreet had put him through so many years ago.

When he put a broad hand on her waist, in an outwardly proprietary manner, Lorelei felt a surge of warmth, even though she knew the gesture was solely for her mother's benefit. Not that he wasn't entitled, she decided, remembering how badly her mother had treated Michael in those long distant days of their teenage romance.

Neither of her parents had ever made any secret of the fact that Michael O'Malley—despite his famous father—was not the boy they would have chosen for their daughter. They preferred someone from the lofty environs of their own privileged world. A boy with a trust fund, a boy comfortable in Audubon Park drawing rooms. A boy whose roots weren't buried deep in the lush, marshy land of the Louisiana bayou.

To her credit, Maureen's only reaction to viewing her daughter with the man she'd once barred from her home, was a faintly arched brow. She was impeccably groomed in a black cocktail dress. The ash blond hair that was several shades darker than her daughter's was styled in an upsweep that accentuated cheekbones sharp enough to cut glass. A faint scent of oriental gardens emanated from smooth, pale skin that looked as if it had never been exposed to the southern sun.

"Hello, Mother."

Maureen offered a powdered cheek. "Hello, dear." Her gimlet gaze observed Michael over her daughter's head. "Hello, Michael."

He nodded, hating the way this woman could make him feel like a tongue-tied teenager again. Reminding himself that he'd won two medals of commendation before quitting the force, he forced the uncomfortable feeling down and managed a smile he was a very long way from feeling.

"Good evening, Mrs. Longstreet. You're looking well."

"As are you," she replied with obvious surprise.

Mossy green eyes flicked over the navy suit Shayne had insisted he buy. Before his brother had come to town, Michael had owned one eight-year-old suit that he'd drag out whenever he had to testify in court. Now he owned three. Reading the grudging approval in the older woman's gaze, he decided the ridiculous price of the double-breasted suit had been worth it.

"I read about your commendations," Maureen offered. "Your mother must be very proud."

"Yes, ma'am. Of course, I think she was proud of me before I got the medals."

"I'm sure she was." She studied him over the rim of her champagne glass. "Did I read in the paper that you'd quit the police force?"

"Yes, ma'am."

"And now you're a private detective?"

Michael decided, for Lorelei's sake, to ignore the tinge of disapproval he heard in Mrs. Longstreet's tone. "Yes, ma'am."

"Is your work like I see on all those television programs? All racing cars and shooting guns?"

"Not really. Since we deal mostly in private security—"

She pounced on that like a sleek Siamese cat upon a fat mouse. "Private security?"

Damn. Michael could have shot himself. That's what he got for allowing this woman to get under his skin. He was usually much more circumspect.

Not wanting to whet Maureen Longstreet's interest regarding his appearance tonight with her daughter, Michael was trying to think of a way to crawl out of the hole he'd dug for himself when Lorelei came to his rescue. "Is Dad here?"

"Unfortunately, your father's at a medical conference in San Francisco." The relief Michael felt at not having to face Dr. Longstreet was short-lived. "He'll be back Friday evening. Of course we'll expect you for dinner," she added.

"Michael and I would love to come," Lorelei said with a smooth, practiced smile.

Although he knew it was perverse of him, Michael enjoyed watching the cloud that moved across Maureen Longstreet's aristocratic features when she realized that he'd be coming to dinner as well.

"Then it's settled." Her smile was as brittle as the crystal glass in her manicured hand. "We'll be looking forward to seeing you." Her cool gaze met Michael's. "Both of you."

That said, she turned and walked away.

"You know," Michael mused, "back in the old days, when I was on the force, I got used to the idea that whenever I went to work, I could face a bullet. But I gotta tell you, sweetheart, I'd rather go after the Norluns mob's nastiest hit man, and all his henchmen, than get stabbed by your mother's stiletto look."

The idea of this man being afraid of anything or anyone made Lorelei laugh.

"It's not funny," he complained. "She made me feel about eighteen again."

"She wasn't looking at you as if you were a teenager," Lorelei assured him. "Actually, I think she found you quite dashing, Michael."

*Dashing?* Michael didn't think he'd ever live long

enough to have that term—which fit Shayne to a tee, he grudgingly admitted—applied to him.

"I think you misinterpreted her reaction."

Lorelei folded her arms and gave him a long, assessing look, from his dark hair down his muscular body to the tips of his shoes, which he'd polished to a sheen that any marine drill sergeant would have envied.

"No," she said with a slow, shake of her head, "I don't think so." Mindless of the fact that they were in a public place, she lifted her hand to his chest. "You really do look quite handsome tonight, Michael. I believe my mother was more than a little impressed."

His grunt suggested he still thought she was wrong. But as he gave her a long masculine appraisal of his own, Lorelei, who was watching him carefully, couldn't miss the rise of hunger in those midnight dark eyes.

Her fingers seemed to be branding him through the suit jacket and starched shirt. Although it suddenly felt as if they were the only two people in the room, on some distant level, Michael was aware that they were drawing attention to themselves.

Even as he reminded himself that he was being well paid to act as a bodyguard for this woman, his personal feelings steamrollered over his professional ones.

He lifted his hand to hers and linked their fingers together. "How much longer do you need to hang around here?"

His voice had deepened, and it skimmed along her nerve endings in a way designed to instill feminine awareness. "I think I've done my part." She smiled, accepting the invitation she heard in his husky voice, viewed in his fathomless eyes. "And I do have an early call tomorrow. It'd probably be a good idea to go back to the hotel and go to bed."

Michael knew she was not talking about going to bed alone. He reminded himself that what he was about to do would be the most unprofessional thing he'd ever done, but right now he didn't much care.

"Wouldn't want you to miss your beauty sleep," he agreed. The energy between them was palpable; Michael was amazed that sparks weren't arcing all around the room.

His hand still entwined with hers, he led her deftly through the crowd. If he thought they'd be able to escape unnoticed, he was wrong. By the time they reached the wide double doors at the end of the room, Lorelei had been intercepted by numerous members of the New Orleans social elite, all of whom professed to be fans.

"You're a popular lady," he said, as they drove back to the hotel.

"I'm the flavor of the month.... Okay," she admitted, as he gave her a wry sideways look, "perhaps the flavor of the year. But fame is a quicksilver thing. Hard to capture and impossible to hold on to."

"And fame's important to you." It was not a question.

"Actually, it's not. You know that all I ever wanted to do was act. Unfortunately, things like tonight seem to come with the territory."

"Must be rough, being fawned over by the rich and famous."

Lorelei didn't like the sarcastic edge to his tone. "Actually, it isn't all it's cracked up to be. You can't possibly believe that I like being stalked by some lunatic."

It was, Michael knew all too well, another thing that unfortunately seemed to come with the territory.

"It's partly because of things like tonight that encourage the guy."

"Excuse me?" Her voice took on the icy tone he was accustomed to hearing from her mother. "Surely I misunderstood you. You didn't really accuse me of encouraging him?"

"Not intentionally. But you're too easygoing, Lorelei. Too accessible."

"I'm not going to allow the creep to force me into a cage." But it was, of course, exactly what had happened. She was every bit as much a prisoner as if she'd been locked away in some jail cell. "I'm going to live as normal a life as possible."

He snorted at that. "I hate to burst your bubble, sweetheart, but going to a cocktail reception sponsored by the mayor is not exactly a normal life for most people."

"True. And you know I didn't want to do it, but—"

"That's exactly my point."

She folded her arms and exhaled a deep, frustrated breath. "If there was a point, I'm afraid I missed it."

"You didn't want to go to that reception tonight.

And, after the day you had, not to mention tomorrow's shooting schedule, you shouldn't have to."

"Eric set it up. I didn't have a choice."

"Of course you did. You could have told him no."

Lorelei thought about that. "He promised the mayor."

"The guy had no right to do that without asking you first."

"I know, but once he had—"

"You felt you had no choice but to bail him out."

"Well, yes."

"Little Miss Perfect Lorelei," he drawled. "After all these years, after all you've accomplished, I would have thought you'd outgrown trying to please everyone."

The accusation stung. "There's nothing wrong with being thoughtful."

"That depends on your definition. Face it, Lorelei, you showed up at that party tonight because you didn't want to disappoint a self-centered guy who wouldn't know the meaning of the word *thoughtful*. A guy who, from what I can tell, hasn't done a damn thing to deserve such loyalty."

"Eric's a friend."

"That's undoubtedly why he decided to scare you to death today, then drag you out in the rain to show you off like some show horse he's just bought. I gotta tell you, sweetheart, if that's how friends treat each other in Tinseltown, I'm glad I stayed here in the delta."

"Eric is one of my closest friends," she insisted again. "That's why he hired you to protect me."

"He hired me to protect you to protect his damn film."

Lorelei hated the fact that he was right. "That, too. But you still haven't explained how my appearing at that party tonight encouraged my stalker."

"Honey, the sight of you in that dress is enough to make any man think of dragging you off to the nearest bed." He'd been thinking of little else since she'd first come out of her bedroom. "But my point, which I'll admit I've wandered from, is that it's a proven fact that stars who tend to get stalked are the ones who are perceived as friendly. Open. Accessible."

Although she was still seething, Lorelei stopped being angry long enough to think about that surprising statement. "Is that true?"

"Absolutely. But to be perfectly honest, your going to that party tonight probably didn't make that much of a difference. Since we've already narrowed the list of suspects down to someone working on the movie, whoever your stalker is already knows your personality. It's undoubtedly too late for you to pull off a complete 180 degree temperament turnaround, even if you could."

He frowned, thinking about the fact that the guy was undoubtedly someone working on the film, which meant that he could have been one of the three men at the party tonight. He'd watched them—Taylor, Wilder, Nelson—and although the first two had registered masculine admiration the minute she'd walked into the banquet room, that wasn't so surprising. After all, he'd spent a good part of the evening wondering what, if anything, she was wearing beneath that body-skimming bit of crystal-studded silk. The fact that Nelson hadn't responded only proved he was definitely gay. But that didn't necessarily preclude his being the stalker, despite the sexual content of the letters.

One of the problems Michael was having with any of those men being the perpetrator was that stalkers, as a rule, tended to have very low self-esteem. Something that could not be said for any of those three men.

"I don't want you to think I'm prying," he said. "But I have to ask you if you've ever been involved with Taylor or Wilder."

"Involved? As in, have I had an affair with either of them?"

"Or maybe just a one-night fling."

She shot him an indignant look. "I don't have one-night flings."

From her tight tone he knew she was telling the truth. Michael wasn't about to admit her denial came as a relief. "Good for you," he said mildly. "How about an affair?"

"Despite what you may have read about wild and hot location romances, I have a hard and fast rule about sleeping with people I work with."

"I take it that's a no."

"Gee, aren't you clever? With deductive skills like that I'm not surprised you decided to become a detective."

He ignored her sarcasm. "Have you ever implied that after the movie was over you might be willing to enter into a relationship?"

"Of course not. We're friends, nothing more." She frowned. "Actually, not even friends. More friendly acquaintances."

"Some of the things Wilder says to you are more than friendly."

Lorelei felt the color flood into her cheeks and was frustrated by the way Michael could put her on the defensive. And angry by the way he could make her feel like a nervous teenager.

"Brian flirts. He seems to think being one of the hottest writers in the business makes him irresistible to women."

"I imagine it doesn't hurt."

"I imagine it doesn't."

"I'd also imagine that some actresses might be willing to sleep with the guy to get him to write a part for them into one of his screenplays."

"I wouldn't be surprised. But he never asked and I certainly never volunteered. We have a symbiotic relationship. He can get more money for a script if I agree to star in it, while at the same time, just being in a Brian Wilder film gives me a cachet that boosts my career. There's no way either of us would want to mess that up by screwing around."

"That's a very businesslike attitude."

"Making movies may look glamorous, but it *is* a business. The people who survive are the ones who remember that."

"Good point." He glanced over at her. "So, if you didn't work with the guy, would you be attracted to him?"

Lorelei wondered if Michael could possibly be jealous and was surprised to discover that she hoped he was. "Are you asking as a private detective?"

"No." He pulled into the parking garage, maneuvered the car into a narrow slot, cut the engine, then turned toward her. "I'm asking as a man who once asked you to marry him."

He wasn't touching her. Not really. His fingers were merely playing with the ends of her hair. But as his knuckles brushed against the bare flesh of her shoulders, Lorelei felt as if he'd touched a sparkler to her warming skin.

She'd thought she'd changed. Surely, after all these years, and all she'd experienced, she'd left behind that idealistic young girl who'd dreamed of white knights in shining armor riding up on prancing stallions to carry her off to their castles. Correction. One white knight. And his name had always been Michael O'Malley.

He leaned toward her, his eyes on hers, his intentions clear. As she felt her lips part in automatic response, Lorelei was reminded, not for the first time since returning to New Orleans, that some things— like her feelings for this man—had not changed even a little bit.

"No," she said softly, her trembling voice little more than a whisper. "Brian is a very good-looking man, in a cute Tom Cruise sort of way. But I'm more attracted to the tall, dark and dangerous types."

"Dangerous?" He arched a brow.

"Dangerous." She touched a hand to his cheek and felt the muscle tense beneath her fingertips. "Dangerous to my mind." Her fingers stroked the side of his chiseled face. "Dangerous to my heart." Down his neck. "And incredibly dangerous to my body." Her free hand took hold of his and lifted it to her left breast. "Feel what you do to me," she invited, her voice a rich ribbon of warmth. "I think I must be having a heart attack."

He smiled as he felt the runaway pounding beneath his fingers. A wild, out-of-control rhythm that matched his own. "Join the club." He lifted their joined hands to his lips. "I want you."

"I know." Her smile was the faintest bit shaky, reminding Michael of the sweet, innocent Lorelei he'd once known. And loved. "And you don't have to be a detective to figure out that I want you, too."

It would be so easy, Michael thought. A few steps to the private elevator, a few more seconds to ride to the penthouse, and then he could make all the dreams and fantasies he'd been tortured by for years a reality.

And then what? What, he asked himself, would change?

Not a damned thing.

"There's just one problem." He released her hand and thrust his own through his hair in a gesture of frustration Lorelei had come to recognize.

"I don't want to think about problems," she said softly. "Not tonight."

He would have had to have been deaf not to hear the invitation, and the plea, in her dulcet tones. Once again the rebellious little voice in the back of his mind reminded Michael how easy it would be to make love to Lorelei. Another, stronger voice reminded him of all the reasons he couldn't do exactly what his body—not to mention his mind and heart—had been aching to do since she'd exited that jetway.

"Better tonight than tomorrow morning." He suspected he was going to hate himself in the morning. But not nearly as badly as he would if he gave in to temptation. "What you said about not playing around where you work..." He paused. "I've always had the same rule."

Lorelei didn't believe that. "You met Desiree when you were investigating her stalker."

"True. But we didn't get together until the guy was behind bars."

Lorelei gave him a long look. "I almost believe you're telling the truth."

"I'd never lie to you, Lorelei."

"But you wanted her."

Michael was uneasy talking about another woman—a married, pregnant woman, for Pete's sake—while his body was still aching for Lorelei.

"Most men would. But we were friends long before we were lovers."

"And now you're friends again." Lorelei frowned as she remembered the shared embrace.

Michael wondered if that was jealousy he heard in her voice, and knew he was in deep trouble when he hoped it was. "A man can't have too many friends."

"Nor can a woman." The mood was fading. Lorelei could feel it slipping away. "Is that what you're saying? That you only want to be friends?"

Did she think he was nuts? "Hell, no." He resisted the urge to drag her into his arms, kiss her hard and deep and long and drive her as crazy as she'd been driving him. "What I'm trying to say, obviously very badly, is that I think it'd be better to practice restraint. For now."

Lorelei remembered, all too clearly, how she'd always hated the way Michael had of always being right.

"Anyone ever tell you that you're too old to be a Boy Scout, O'Malley?"

Michael threw back his head and laughed.

"Believe me, sweetheart," he said, as he opened the driver's door, "I'm about as far from being a Boy Scout as you can get."

As he walked around to open her door, Lorelei, who'd gotten out of the habit of expecting such southern gentleman gestures, considered that he might not exactly be a Boy Scout. But Michael O'Malley was still the closest thing to a knight in shining armor she'd ever known.

DAMN HER! The man sat in the dark, watching as she and the bodyguard walked hand in hand to the parking garage elevator, her dress like a silver beacon in the darkness of the underground parking area. Of all the women in Hollywood, she was the one he'd always believed to be pure of heart. Which was why he'd chosen her for his beloved. She was the only woman he'd ever met who could soothe the searing pain in his breast and calm the roaring in his head. He'd always considered her an anomaly for Hollywood: a good, pure girl with a golden heart.

In the beginning he'd even allowed himself to believe that she was a virgin. A virgin who'd saved herself just for him.

But ever since coming to New Orleans, she'd begun to show her true colors. Before her arrival in the Big Easy, her social life had resembled that of a cloistered nun. But suddenly, it was as if she were a particularly colorful snake who'd shed its skin, revealing the ugliness inside. He'd watched her with the detective tonight, watched their exchanged glances, casual touches, lingering looks, and he knew that they were sleeping together. There was even a chance, he thought again, given how carefree she'd been while shopping for that too revealing dress with Shayne O'Malley, that she was sleeping with the Incredible Hulk's brother, as well.

Despite the damning evidence against her, he'd been trying to keep an open mind, trying to give her the benefit of the doubt. But as he watched the elevator door close, the elevator that would take them up to the suite, where they would no doubt undress each other, then spend the night in a fevered frenzy, he was forced to accept the unpalatable fact that the woman he'd put on a pedestal, his own vestal virgin, so to speak, was just another common ordinary piece of Hollywood trash.

Bile rose in his throat as pictures of Lorelei with the detective writhed in his mind like poisonous snakes. He opened the door to his rental car and threw up the rich canapes and champagne onto the concrete floor. Then, his stomach empty, his mind cleansed and his blood cooled, he turned the key in the ignition. As he drove out of the garage, the man began to plot his revenge.

# 9

LORELEI WAS RELIEVED when the next three days went
smoothly. To her surprise, she began to become accustomed to being with Michael. She found that she enjoyed his company, enjoyed talking with him about
everything and nothing, enjoyed looking up after
shooting a scene to find him watching her with open
admiration, enjoyed him practicing her lines—which,
predictably, Brian kept changing—with her back at
the hotel at night.

Although no one could ever convince her that she
and Michael hadn't been truly in love, they'd never
been lovers. Thinking back on it, Lorelei decided that
raging hormones and the rampant insecurities that
personified everyone's teenage years, had also kept
them from being friends.

The fact that they could be close friends now was as
pleasing as it was surprising. In fact, although she'd
always hated exercise, and only did it to keep her
curves in control, she found that one of the high points
of each day was running with Michael in the morning.
Even if she hated to think what the daily stop for beignets was doing to her waistline.

But she wasn't going to worry about her weight. After all, she was only going to be in New Orleans a few

more days, Lorelei reminded herself. Then she'd return to her real life in Los Angeles, and her uncharacteristic indulgence in the delicious, deep fried southern donuts and the rest of the local fare Michael had been coaxing her into eating would become merely a fond memory.

Along with the sound of jazz floating on the sultry perfumed night air, the jingle of the harness bells on the horses that pulled the tourist carriages around the French Quarter, and the low deep tones of the paddlewheel boat whistles on the wide Mississippi.

Unfortunately, she'd also be leaving Michael behind.

"What's the matter?"

Lorelei hadn't realized that she'd sighed until she heard his voice. She shook her head and forced a smile. "Nothing."

Michael had never been one to let things drop unsettled. "Are you worried about your upcoming scene?"

They were on the way to the bar where the stripper scene she'd been dreading was to be filmed. This time she didn't even try to stifle her sigh. "I'm not wild about the idea," she admitted. "But Eric thinks it's pivotal."

"Pivotal." Michael chewed that one over. "That's a new term for *gratuitous sex.*"

Since she'd come to value his opinion, Lorelei turned toward him. "Do you really think it's gratuitous?"

He shrugged, wishing he'd just kept his mouth

shut. What the hell did he know about the movie business? Lorelei had built an enviable career playing the siren. Who was he to criticize, even if the thought of her taking off her clothes today had kept him awake all last night.

"Hey," he said, wanting to apologize for making a tough day even harder, "if Eric says it's pivotal, he's probably right. After all, every movie you've ever made with him has been a box office smash."

"I didn't realize you kept track of things like that." She decided she liked the idea of him having read about her, thought about her, during their time apart.

"I don't really. I told you, I did my research after Shayne took this case."

"Oh." So he hadn't been thinking about her after all.

"And if this movie turns out half as good as *Hot Ice*, you undoubtedly have another hit on your hands."

"You saw *Hot Ice*?" Despite all the sexy scenes in that film, she'd been proud of her work, pleased that she'd been able to create a character with more layers, more depth, than Brian had conceived when he'd written the role.

"About a dozen times." His grin was quick, warm and faintly self-conscious. "You were terrific. The way you portrayed that cat burglar's internal conflicts made her a remarkably sympathetic character. I could see how the cop couldn't help but get involved. Even knowing ahead of time that there was no safe way out of the relationship."

"Thank you." Nothing he could have said would have given her more pleasure. The compliment, easily stated and seemingly genuine, warmed her. "What about you?" she asked as they paused to let a clutch of tourists pass in front of the car. "You are, without a doubt, the most straight-arrow man I've ever known. Could you see yourself falling for a woman like that?"

"In a heartbeat." His grin faded. His expression was as serious as she'd ever seen it and from the lambent fire gleaming in his midnight blue eyes, Lorelei realized that they were no longer talking about her fictional cat burglar.

Her mouth went suddenly dry. She swallowed. "We need to talk."

"I'd say it's about time." Past time, Michael amended, thinking of all the things he'd spent years wishing he'd said. Better late than never, he decided.

"The problem is that I can't focus on today's shoot while I'm all mixed up about us."

At least she was willing to admit that there was an *us*. That, Michael decided, was progress. Terrifying, in its own way, since he had no idea where they'd go from here, but it was progress, nevertheless.

"Let's take things one at a time," he suggested. "The first order of business is for you to film today's stripper scene. Then we'll go back to the hotel and order an early dinner. And talk afterward."

She'd been waiting over a decade to learn why he'd dumped her. And, although it no longer stung, there'd been a time when Lorelei had fantasized about making him crawl. However, now that she'd been given another chance with this man, she wasn't going to wallow in the past. They'd discuss it, like the two intelligent, rational adults they'd grown up to be. Then they'd put it behind them and move on with their lives.

Which, of course, only presented another set of problems. Even supposing Michael *did* want a future together, how willing would he be to go through life as Mr. Lorelei Longstreet?

Talk about quantum leaps, she thought. Although she knew that Michael truly cared for her and had no doubts at all that he wanted to go to bed with her, nothing he'd done or said had even hinted that he might be thinking of ever-afters.

You're hopeless, Lorelei scolded herself. You're behaving the same way you did back in high school when you used to write his name all over your folder. She'd thought she'd grown up. Obviously, when it came to Michael O'Malley, she'd always be sixteen years old.

"Well, we're here."

Jerked from her mental turmoil, Lorelei looked up at the gaudy Bourbon Street nightclub that had been booked for the film crew to use for the next six hours. At her insistence, the cocktail waitresses and dancers who usually worked during the day were being paid double the wages and tips they could expect to make during their lost shifts. Eric had laughed at her, accusing her of being a bleeding heart liberal. Lorelei hadn't denied the charge. But she had stuck to her guns.

"I guess I may as well get it over with."

"I guess so." Michael sounded no more eager than she.

Lorelei suddenly realized why she'd been so worried about this scene. It wasn't as if she'd played a nun in her other movies. She'd certainly had her share of bedroom and shower scenes. Especially during her first year in the business, when she'd played a conniving soap opera vixen who'd slept with seemingly the entire male population of Pine Valley.

But never had Michael O'Malley been watching from the sidelines. And that, she realized, made all the difference.

"You understand that it's not me, don't you?" She turned to him, taking hold of his arms. "That it's just a role I'm playing? That when I'm up there, it isn't really going to be *me* stripping."

Her expression was as earnest as he'd ever seen it. Beneath his jacket, her nails were biting into his arms. "Give me some credit, Lorelei. I know the difference between acting and real life."

"So, you're not going to be jealous?"

He laughed at that. A rich, bold masculine laugh that dispelled the tension hovering over them like a thunderhead. "I'm a detective, sweetheart. Not a saint. Of course I'm going to be jealous as hell. I also intend to put every guy in that club today on notice."

"On notice?"

"They can look. But they can't touch. Any one of them who makes a move to lay a finger on my girl is going to get shot."

My girl. Once again the sixteen-year-old girl's heart that was still lurking inside her began doing somersaults. "You'd never do that."

"Want to bet?" He wasn't smiling. But Lorelei knew he was kidding. He had to be. Wasn't he?

While her mind was still struggling with that question, without warning, Michael's head swooped down and he covered her mouth with his.

The sparks, which had been smoldering silently for so many years, instantly flared to life. Lorelei's tumbling thoughts disintegrated, vaporized by the heat of Michael's lips, the burning touch of his broad hand as it slipped under her cropped cotton sweater, touching her in the way she'd been aching to be touched for days.

His lips scorched hers; his tongue dove deep, drawing a shuddering moan. As he pulled her against him, heat to heat, Lorelei was caught up in a furnace blast of fire and steam.

Kissing Lorelei was like a roller coaster ride down memory lane. She was everything Michael remembered her to be, and more. When she'd been younger, she'd tasted sweet, like forbidden fruit. During the intervening years she'd ripened to a lush, heady maturity.

She tasted as effervescent as the champagne she was undoubtedly accustomed to drinking in Hollywood, as rich as imported cognac, more dangerous than a bottle of the moonshine his uncle Claude used to make out in the bayou.

She was in his system, making him drunk. Perhaps, what he'd been thinking night after sleepless night was true: she'd always been there.

He didn't want to ever stop kissing her, he wanted

to strip the sweater and jeans off her lush body. He wanted to claim her for his own, which was what he should have done years ago before she got on that damn plane that had taken her away from him. But Michael forced his mind to cool.

"If we keep this up," he muttered, dragging his mouth from her lips to nuzzle at her fragrant neck, "we're going to get arrested."

"That's okay." Her hair rippled down her back as she tilted her head back, luxuriating in the warmth of the caress. "Surely you have friends on the force."

"Friends who'd get a kick out of busting me for a 288."

Deciding to take turns, she pressed her open mouth against his neck. "What's a 288?"

"An L and L." When she touched the tip of her tongue to the vein throbbing beneath his jaw, Michael groaned. "Lewd and lascivious." Did she know she was driving him crazy? Of course she did, he decided as her tongue continued to trail a wet swathe down his burning skin. "Not to mention the ever popular 311...indecent exposure."

She felt him tremble and experienced a surge of feminine power stronger than anything she'd ever felt before. "Neither of us is indecent."

"Not yet." He took hold of her shoulders and put her a little away from him. "But if you keep kissing me like that, I'm not going to be responsible for what happens."

"Pooh." She smiled at him. With her mouth and her

wide, silvery eyes. "You're the most responsible man I've ever met, Michael."

He hated hearing that. It made him sound boring. Dull. Which, Michael allowed reluctantly, he probably was, compared to those high-living L.A. hotshots she was used to dating.

He sighed and ran his hand down her hair. "We'd better get in there."

"I suppose we should." She'd never been late for a call in her career. But never had she had less incentive to move from where she was.

They entered the bar, his hand lightly on her back in the possessive way she'd grown accustomed to. Michael tried to tell himself he was imagining the anticipation sparking the humid air, but watching the male eyes follow Lorelei as she disappeared into the ladies' room, which had been designated a dressing room and which Michael had already checked out and declared secure, he knew that every guy in the place was waiting to watch Lorelei strip.

The thought was not an encouraging one. Tamping down the jealousy, Michael concentrated on trying to figure out which of the men on this set today was Lorelei's stalker. Unfortunately, the suspects made up a very long list.

"Okay, boys and girls," Eric called out, "we're getting ready to roll. Quiet on the set."

"Quiet on the set," the assistant director echoed. "Scene thirty-six, take one. Rolling."

Michael had read the script. He'd even, in an uncharacteristically masochistic mood, envisioned Lorelei acting out the role of the sexy mystery writer turned undercover stripper. But even so, there was no way he could have been prepared for the reality of the scene.

There was a sound of a motorcycle gunning its engine offstage. Every male in the room was at attention, reminding Michael of Elvis, his old hunting dog, at point.

The engine roared louder. Then, while everyone watched, Lorelei, clad in a black leather jacket, body-hugging leather shorts and thigh-high boots rode in on a police motorcycle while the actor playing the part of the club's emcee introduced, "Officer Extremely Friendly."

The sight of her long legs straddling that bike was enough to make Michael want to drag her off the stage and away from prying eyes. Unfortunately, he knew that it was only going to get worse.

Which it did.

Flashing a vixen's smile, she climbed off the bike and began moving her hips to the gut-wrenchingly sexy music that a blues band was belting out.

She pulled a prop pistol from the holster she was wearing low on the hip, gunslinger style. No cop would wear his sidearm that way, Michael thought, then decided reality wasn't all that important for the act. She spread her legs, which looked even longer than usual in those gleaming black boots with stiletto hooker heels so high Michael didn't know how she managed to stand up in them, let alone try to dance.

She pointed the gun at the audience. "Freeze suckers!'' There was a rolling drumbeat. When she pulled the trigger, the pistol fired sparks, but no bullets.

Then she got down to business.

Unlike so many of the girls who worked in the Quarter, often dancing in the front windows of the clubs to attract customers, Lorelei did not display all her feminine charms at once. On the contrary, the act gave new meaning to the word *tease.*

The first thing to come off was the brimmed police cap. She plucked it from her hair, which had been crimped into a mass of rippling silver waves by the hairdresser, turned it around three times in her hands, then tossed it into the crowd. An extra Michael recognized as the kid who had delivered pizzas to the crew the day before caught it with a wide grin and put it on his own head.

The fringed leather motorcycle cop gloves were next, and somehow, as she tugged each finger free with her teeth, she made taking off a pair of gloves seem an almost indecent act.

The audience was getting into it now, shouting for her to take off more. Naturally, she obliged, unzipping the leather jacket, revealing a black leather bra with chain straps that offered up eye-grabbing cleavage. Her skin was porcelain pale against the jet leather and sparkled in a way that suggested the makeup woman had dusted some crystal substance onto her shoulders and the crest of her breasts.

Michael didn't know which was harder, watching Lorelei's lascivious movements as she strutted back and forth across the small stage, dragging the jacket behind her, or watching the men in the room watch her.

"Christ," Brian, who was standing beside Michael murmured, "I wrote the damn scene and I'm turned on."

He wasn't the only one. "She's good," Michael allowed.

"Good? Hell, the lady's world-class. By the time she gets down to those pasties, there won't be a guy in the place capable of walking out of here."

Feeling an urge to put his fist into the center of the writer's handsome face, Michael jammed his hands into the back pockets of his jeans to keep them out of trouble.

"Cut," Eric suddenly called out.

"Cut," the assistant director echoed.

The band stopped in the middle of the song's bridge. Standing alone on the stage, Lorelei put her hand to her forehead, shielding her eyes against the glaring klieg lights.

"What's wrong? Please don't tell me I have to start again." Her discomfort with that idea was more than evident.

The metamorphosis was startling, even to Michael, who'd known she'd been acting. One minute she was Officer Extremely Friendly, the sexiest stripper on Bourbon Street; the next minute she was the Lorelei he'd known most of his life. The girl he'd once loved.

"You were doing great, sweetheart," Eric assured her. "But you're not sweating."

"That's because you've got the temperature about

forty degrees in here," she complained. When she wrapped her arms around herself, the always vigilant wardrobe mistress suddenly appeared with a silk robe.

"I instructed the electrician to lower the temperature so your makeup wouldn't melt under the lights," Eric said. "But I want you to look hot and sweaty."

"I can do many things on cue, Eric," Lorelei said dryly. "Scream, cry, even faint. But sweating on command is beyond the scope of my talent."

"No problem." He called for the makeup woman, who appeared on the scene with a plastic water bottle. Sighing, Lorelei surrendered the robe, held out her arms, and turned slowly while the woman spritzed a mixture of water and baby oil onto her skin.

"That's better," Eric said, nodding his satisfaction with the effect. "Okay," he cued the band and Lorelei, "let's pick it up a few bars before we broke off."

"Scene thirty-six," the assistant director called out. "Take two. Rolling."

As much as Michael hated to admit it, the director was right. Before, she'd appeared strangely alien, like some sort of unearthly goddess. But the moisture glistening above her vermilion lips, between her breasts, on her torso above the low-cut waistband of the skin-hugging shorts and on the sleek flesh at the inside of her thighs made her appear far more human. And, although Michael never would have thought it possible, even sexier.

She turned her back to the audience, smiling at them over her shoulder. It was then he noticed, for the first time, that the dazzling smile didn't quite reach her eyes. Michael wondered if such mental detachment was her way of showing the fictional character's discomfort with what she was forced to do to research her mystery story, or Lorelei's own unease.

She unfastened the bra and turned back to the cameras, holding it coyly against her breasts, the thin chain straps flashing silver in the blue spotlight focused on her. Although it was impossible to hear much of anything over the blaring music, Michael imagined he heard a collective intake of breath as every man in the club waited for that bit of black leather to drop.

And then something filtered into his consciousness. A faint cracking sound coming from above the stage. Acting on impulse, he shouted, took the six steps on to the stage two at a time, and flung himself against her, sending her flying. A moment later, a huge kleig light crashed to the floor, only inches from where Lorelei had been standing.

# 10

THE ACTION WAS SO fleeting it took onlookers several seconds to catch up. The band continued playing, while the musicians dwindled off one at a time as comprehension dawned. A murmured question rippled through the crowd, turning into a babble of excitement as what had happened—and even worse, what could have happened—sank in.

"Dammit," Eric shouted, pushing his way to the stage, "what the hell happened here?"

"What does it look like?" Brian said, his shaky voice revealing heightened emotion. "O'Malley just saved Lorelei's life." He took to the stage as well and crouched down beside Lorelei, who was still lying beneath Michael.

"How are you?" Brian asked her.

"I think I'm fine," Lorelei managed to gasp even as her heart continued to pound in her ears. "Although I'm having a little trouble breathing."

That could be because his chest was crushing hers, Michael realized. She felt small and soft beneath him. And he also couldn't help noticing that she felt damn good, too.

"Sorry," he mumbled, rolling off her. At the same time, he pulled the pistol from his shoulder holster.

"Good God," Eric said, backing up when he saw the gun.

"Is that really necessary?" Brian asked.

"Yeah." His own heart pounding in a way that made Michael think he might be having a heart attack, he pulled the flip cell phone from his jacket pocket and hit the fast dial number for his office.

"Get down here to Le Girls Cabaret," he said abruptly when Shayne answered. "Yeah, she's okay. But we had a close call and I want to get her back to the hotel while you start questioning people here." He paused and considered his options. "You'd better call Dirkson down at the cop shop and have him send some guys over, too."

"You're calling in the police?" Eric asked. "Is that really necessary?"

Michael looked down at Lorelei, who was sitting on the stage, her arms wrapped around herself, looking somewhat shell-shocked now that the adrenaline jolt was beginning to subside.

"Your star was almost killed," he replied. "I'd say that yeah, that calls for the cops."

"Surely you're not implying it wasn't an accident," Brian said, appearing honestly shocked by the suggestion that someone had actually tried to harm Lorelei. "I mean, I know she's been having problems with some lovesick fan, but everyone knows those guys never act on their fantasies."

Michael wanted to throttle him. "Don't tell me, you researched stalkers for a script."

"*Dangerous Passions*," Brian said defensively.

"I saw it. And, while it may have worked as entertainment, it wasn't an accurate portrayal of the problem. You must not have run across the little fact that before John Hinckley, Jr. tried to assassinate the president, he wrote a letter to Jodie Foster telling her that fantasies can become reality in his world. I guess everyone saw the proof of that a few days later, over and over again on their televisions."

He heard Lorelei's sharp intake of breath and realized that he'd scared her. Which, Michael decided, wasn't all that bad. Although she'd professed unease about her stalker, and had reluctantly allowed Taylor to hire a bodyguard, he'd sensed that the very real danger hadn't really hit home. Now that it had, it was up to him to assure her that he'd keep her safe. Then he had to somehow live up to his word.

"Even so," Eric argued, "accidents do happen."

"Sure they do. But until we prove differently, I'm not taking any chances." He reholstered the gun, then turned to the wardrobe mistress and asked for the robe, which was immediately handed over. Kneeling down, he wrapped it around Lorelei's ice-cold shoulders. As he was helping her to her feet, Shayne walked in, followed by two men in jeans and T-shirts Michael recognized from his days on the force. One was his former partner, who greeted him with a grim expression.

"Come on, sweetheart," Michael said, putting his arm around Lorelei's shoulders, "Shayne's arrived with the cavalry. We can get you out of here."

She was trembling. Her teeth began to chatter from

the chill that had crept over her, a chill that went all the way to the bone.

"It'll be okay," Michael assured her yet again once they were alone in his car. "*You'll* be okay."

"I know." She hated the way she'd lost control. Her teeth were clacking together as if she were in the Arctic, and her hands and her voice couldn't stop shaking. "I realized something when you were telling Brian about stalkers."

"What?"

"He really could kill me."

"He'd have to go through me, first." Michael slanted her a grin, hoping to win an answering smile. "And I'm a pretty big obstacle."

That was definitely not an exaggeration. Remembering the way every bone in her body had rattled when he'd hit her and knocked her to the stage, Lorelei figured that she'd have bruises for a week.

"I owe you, O'Malley," she murmured. "Big time."

"You don't owe me a thing."

His jaw was set, his eyes were chips of cobalt ice. Lorelei had always thought of Michael as the steady, easygoing, albeit stubborn, brother. Now she caught a glimpse of the steely man who'd made a career of hunting down stalkers and serial killers and realized that in his own way, Michael could be as dangerous as her stalker.

"I suppose this is where you point out that you were only doing your job."

This time the look he shot her was laced with disgust. "You know better than that."

Yes, she did. What he'd done had nothing to do with the fact he'd been paid to do it, but everything to do with the fact that deep down inside, Michael O'Malley had the heart of a hero. He was undoubtedly genetically incapable of turning his back on anyone who might need his help. "I still owe you."

Michael wondered when she'd gotten so damn stubborn. The girl he remembered had been soft-hearted and far more malleable. He'd always known that in spite of her burning desire to act, all it would have taken to keep her in New Orleans was for him to ask her not to go to California. She would have stayed. And, he reminded himself, would have ended up resenting him for the rest of her life.

And, although it'd make his job easier if he could just talk her into going into hiding until they could catch the pervert who'd obviously become obsessed to the point of murder, Michael decided that he liked the strong brave woman she'd become.

"You can repay me by getting Wilder to cut that scene from the film," he said.

She glanced over at him. Surprise had made her momentarily forget her fear. "So you still think it's gratuitous?"

He shrugged as he pulled into the hotel parking garage. "I don't know about that. But I do know that it's about the hottest thing you've ever done and if I have to watch it again, we're going to be in deep trouble."

"Why?"

"Because I really will have no choice but to shoot

every sex-crazed guy in the place for what they're thinking."

"How do you know what they'll be thinking?"

"Because it's the same thing any red-blooded male would be thinking watching you strut your stuff like that."

"Oh... Were you thinking those thoughts today?"

"You know damn well I was."

A slow warmth spread through her, burning off a bit of the deep chill. "Good."

Michael's only answer, as he parked in the reserved space next to the VIP elevator, was a muttered curse.

Although she considered herself a modern, independent woman, Lorelei uttered not a single objection as Michael ushered her into the gilt-and-marble bathroom and sat her down on the velvet dressing table bench while he ran hot water into a tub nearly large enough to swim laps in. As she watched his strong dark hands open the cut crystal bottle and shake the perfumed bath salts into the water, Lorelei was struck with a sudden urge to drag him down onto the plush sea green carpet and have her way with him. Or better yet, pull him into the sunken, tiled bathtub that seemed to be designed for two.

"Okay," he said, oblivious to her thoughts as he turned back to her. "Can you get out of those clothes by yourself?"

Wondering what he'd say if she asked for his help, Lorelei remembered what he'd said about his rule about not mixing work and pleasure. Unwilling to risk rejection when too many of her nerve endings were still jangling, she reminded herself that discretion was supposed to be the better part of valor.

"I'll be fine. Really," she insisted when he appeared to doubt her. "These clothes were designed to strip off easily."

"Don't remind me," he muttered. Before she could object, he bent down, took hold of her ankle, and lifted her foot. Holding it against the front of his jeans, he unzipped the black leather boot, pulled it off, then did the same with the other foot. "You looked like every biker's private fantasy up there."

Once again, Lorelei thought about making love with Michael, positive that it was the one thing that could help her forget what had happened earlier. He'd always been able to make her body float and her mind drift. And dear heaven, how she needed to shut her mind off.

Lorelei moistened her lips. "Should I take that as a compliment?"

Her voice, which had trembled earlier, had turned sultry. The throaty tones strummed now familiar inner chords. She suddenly looked about as innocent as a smoking 9mm pistol, making Michael wonder if she could actually recover so quickly, or if she was acting for his benefit.

Resisting an urge to press his mouth against the arch of the slender foot tipped with toenails painted a gleaming pearlescent that reminded him of sunshine on snowdrifts, Michael nearly swore as he released her.

"Obviously, you're feeling better."

He looked down at her, innumerable emotions battling inside him. The need to protect warred with the desire to plunder. The need to find her stalker vied with an urge to take her away, far from here where no one could ever find them, perhaps out to the cabin he owned with Roarke and Shayne where he could make love to her over and over again until the rest of the world went away.

Lorelei watched the shutters go down over Michael's eyes, viewed the unreadable expression on his face and realized that the man was every bit as strong willed as he'd been when he was younger. Worse, she decided as she felt the tight pressure around her heart. Not wanting him to realize that he had the power to hurt her, she reminded herself that she'd been on her own since she was sixteen years old, and had carved out a place for herself in a fiercely competitive world. She was no longer the wide-eyed virgin who'd worn her young and open heart on her sleeve.

She could handle this, Lorelei assured herself. She could handle finishing this film she wished she'd never agreed to make; she could handle her unruly feelings for Michael. She could even handle her stalker.

Oh, God. When had she become such a liar?

"I'll be fine," she said softly.

He'd watched the play of emotions march across her expressive face, realized that she was still more upset than she was willing to admit, but decided that she was also strong enough to come through this with all flags flying.

"Of course you will." Because he wanted to take her in his arms and promise that he'd keep her safe always, Michael backed away from temptation. "Call if you need anything."

Lorelei watched him walk out of the bathroom, closing the door behind him. Then she lowered her face in her hands and began to sob silently, giving in to the earlier shock and her turmoiled emotions.

Finally, she was cried out. The fragrant steam rising from the bathtub drew her like a siren's song, promising warmth and comfort. Pushing herself to her feet, she took off the rest of the ridiculous Officer Extremely Friendly stripper costume, vowing to burn it at the first opportunity.

She was leaning against the puffy bath pillow, luxuriating in the way the warm water soothed her nerves and numbed her mind when a knock on the bathroom door jerked her from a daydream of making love with Michael on a sun-drenched Tahitian beach.

"Come in."

Michael was hit with the sultry scent as soon as he opened the door. The room was as fragrant and steamy as a tropical rain forest and the sight of her, up to her shoulders in a thick layer of frothy iridescent bubbles, her pale hair pinned haphazardly atop her head, was enough to drive any man mad. Michael almost swallowed his tongue.

"I thought you might like some tea."

"Thank you." Her smile was warm, but distant. Almost guarded. "In the movies the hero always gives the heroine brandy after the bad guys almost kill her."

"That's in the movies. I figured tea would be better than pouring alcohol on already tattered nerve endings. But I can get some brandy from the minibar, if you'd prefer it."

"No, this is fine." When she held out her hand, bubbles dripped from her bare arm.

He handed her the cup, resisting the urge to pull her out of the silky, perfumed water.

Suppressing an almost overwhelming desire to pull him into the tub with her, Lorelei took a sip. She sighed, as if she'd just tasted ambrosia, rather than sweetened cinnamon-spiced tea.

"This is perfect. Thank you," she said again.

"You're welcome." Knowing that he should leave, now, before they got into trouble, he sat down on the edge of the tub and picked up the loofah sponge from the tile shelf behind the bath pillow. "Turn around. I'll wash your back."

"Gracious." She took another, longer drink of tea, suddenly wishing it *was* something stronger. Her nerves, which had begun to be soothed by the hot water, were tangling all over again. "Is it standard operating procedure to perform such personal services for all the women you're hired to protect?"

He dipped the sponge beneath the layer of suds, then squeezed it in his palm, allowing the water to stream over her shoulder. "You're the first."

Their eyes met. And held. And in that suspended moment, both knew there'd be no turning back.

"Well." Lorelei let out a shaky breath. "In that case, how can I refuse such a gallant offer?"

He moved the rough sponge over the smooth expanse of porcelain flesh and thought about the time he'd flown to Las Vegas to bring back a prisoner. At Caesar's Palace, the night before he was scheduled to pick up the burglar at the county jail, Michael had won ten dollars playing blackjack, lost another twenty in the slots, and had bought two overpriced beers at the Cleopatra's Barge bar. At the time, he'd decided that Vegas was a town for suckers. There was no way a guy could come out a winner.

Now, looking at Lorelei sitting amidst the glistening bubbles, he had the same feeling. When it came to resisting the charms of this woman he'd never really stopped loving, there was no way he could win; the odds were stacked against him.

He dropped his hand.

"Michael?" She looked back over her shoulder, her eyes wide and maddeningly innocent. "Is something wrong?"

He was about to lie to her, to brush off her concern, to assure her that everything was just jim-dandy. Other than some sicko trying to kill her. Along with the salient little fact that he'd been feeling as if he'd stumbled into quicksand from the time she'd first stepped off that plane.

"Yeah...you terrify me," he surprised them both by saying.

"What?" Her shock was not feigned. "*I* terrify *you?*" She hadn't thought anything could ever frighten this man. Looking up at him, taking in his intense, dark eyes and grimly set lips, it was almost impossible to believe how gentle she knew he could be.

"Not you, exactly," he all but growled, reminding her of a cranky lion. "The way you make me feel."

"Ah." Now that she could understand. "News flash, O'Malley," she murmured, running the back of her hand down his steely set jaw. "If we're talking about feelings, then you scare me to death, too."

His heart clenched. Michael tried to remember how to draw air in and out of his lungs. "Perhaps we just ought back off. Get used to the idea."

"We could do that," she agreed quietly. Her hand trailed down his neck, then smoothed over the wide shoulder she felt tense beneath her touch. "Or, you could make love to me. The way I've been dying for you to do."

It would be so damn easy. The problem was, Michael had never trusted anything easy. "Lorelei—"

"You saved my life today, Michael." She pressed her palm against his chest, her eyes held his with the unwavering strength of her need. "Now I need you to help me feel alive again."

"So, I'm to consider this an act of charity?"

Needs were building, higher and more insistent than anything she'd felt before. Lorelei decided if by some inhuman act of will Michael actually managed to resist her seduction efforts, she might truly die. "If it helps you get beyond your stupid rule, I can live with that."

Marveling that she could manage a joke after all she'd been through today, and knowing that there was no way he was going to be able to keep resisting what she wanted—what they both wanted—Michael threw in the towel.

Lorelei sighed. Her arms crept around his neck.

He brushed a kiss at the corner of her mouth. "With all the changes, you taste just the same."

"Tell me." Her lips curved, pleased. "Tell me how I taste."

"I wouldn't think Hollywood's most gorgeous sex goddess would need to dig for compliments."

Rewarded by the humor in his deep voice, Lorelei felt her heart take wings. "All women need compliments, O'Malley." She shivered as his skimming mouth paused at her ear, his teeth nipping gently at the tender lobe. "Even gorgeous sex goddesses."

He touched the tip of his tongue to a sensitive spot behind her ear that no other man had ever discovered. "You want compliments?" He slipped a hand beneath the melting bubbles to cup her breast, the intimate touch causing her to begin trembling all over again. He touched his mouth to hers. "Sometimes you taste like sunshine...like spring rains.... Then there are those other times..."

He released her mouth, watched her tongue slip out to skim lightly over her lips, as if wanting to recapture his taste.

"Other times?" Her heart skipped a beat as he stroked the roughened pad of his thumb over her nipple, while taking her mouth in a longer, deeper, drugging kiss that made her head spin and her bones melt.

"Other times you taste like temptation. Hot and

dark and rich as brandy-spiked chicory coffee." It was his turn to skim his tongue over her lips. Down her throat. "I don't think I'll ever get enough of you, Lorelei."

It was what she'd been waiting to hear. Lorelei kissed him back. A hard, anxious kiss blazing with emotion.

*Take me.* The words echoed in her head like the toll of the warning buoys out in the gulf; there was no need to say them out loud. They shimmered in her sigh, radiated from the fingertips of her slender hands fretting over his shoulders, up and down his back. *Take me.*

Michael readily obliged. He dragged her from the cooling water and holding her against him, chest to chest, thighs to thighs, mouth to mouth, he stumbled out of the bathroom toward the bed.

Not caring that she was dripping all over the carpeting, heedless of the fact that they were about to get the silk smooth Egyptian cotton sheets wet, he fell onto the bed, pulling her with him.

He'd wanted to be gentle. Had planned to take her slowly, to show her that some things were worth waiting for. But needs that had been pent up too long burst free, like a storm-swollen river over the levee. He rolled over, pressing her into the mattress as he took her breast in his mouth. When her shocked gasp filtered through the roaring in his head, Michael struggled to pull back.

"I'm sorry."

"Don't you dare apologize." Her own fingers were

tearing at his shirt, scattering buttons to all the corners of the room. Lorelei tasted passion and reveled in it. She exuded recklessness that fired his own desperate hunger. "I want you, Michael. I've wanted you forever."

She was wild beneath him, every sensuous movement a demand that he take more, go faster. Michael left her only long enough to rip off the shirt she'd torn and rid himself of the rest of his clothes. Then he was back, braceleting both her wrists in one hand, holding them above his head.

His free hand cupped the source of heat, ruthlessly sending her soaring. She peaked instantly, bucking against his touch, her back arched bowstring tight.

Even as she poured over his hand, he was whipping her up again, higher, harder. The second climax left her shuddering, but it still wasn't enough.

"Lorelei."

She murmured something incoherent, tossing her head on the pillow in a way that shook the pins loose and made her hair tumble down over her shoulders and breasts.

"Look at me."

Although it took a herculean effort, she dragged her lids open and found herself staring into an intense blue fire so hot it was almost blinding.

"You're mine." He thrust his fingers into the moist heat, making her cry out as another hot wave swamped her. "You've always been mine."

"Yours." The single word was torn from her throat, a ragged thread of sound. Desperate to touch him, as he was touching her, Lorelei nearly wept with relief when he released her hands.

"Yours," she repeated as she curled her fingers around his sex and made him moan.

Her stroking touch nearly made him explode. There was a clash of teeth as his mouth ate into hers. He dug his fingers into her hips, lifted her up, pulled her warm silk thighs apart to open her fully. Then with a thrust of his hips, he plunged into her, deep and hard, all the way to the hilt.

She cried out again, in pleasure, not pain, then wrapped her long legs around his hips, holding him in a viselike grip as he hammered into her, driving her deeper and deeper into the mattress, every thrust touching her in places no man had ever touched, until they were both engulfed in a white-hot rush of sensation. Her fingers digging into the rigid flesh of his back, Lorelei hung on for dear life as they rode out the storm together.

Feeling as if he'd been turned inside out, Michael collapsed on top of her. Neither of them said a word for a long, long time. There was only the rough sound of unsteady breathing to break the silence. The earthy, redolent scent of their lovemaking mingled with the fragrance of flowers emanating from her damp skin.

"Are we still alive?" Michael asked against her throat.

Lorelei thought about that and decided that the pulsating waves that were still rippling between her legs was a very good sign. "I think so."

"Good." Afraid he was crushing her, he rolled over onto his side, taking her with him.

"Well," she murmured, "that was certainly worth waiting for."

It took what little breath he had left to laugh. "Talk about living up to your billing." He ran a hand down her back, over the tight round curve of her bottom. "You really are terrific."

Lorelei was faintly hurt by his assumption that what they'd just experienced was even vaguely normal for her. Although she didn't really have the energy to argue, she did feel the need to set the record straight.

"It's never been like that before," she said, nuzzling against him.

"Yeah, I imagine most guys would have the control to dry you off first." Now that his head was beginning to clear, Michael became aware of the damp sheets.

"That's not what I mean." It was an effort to get the words out. "I mean that I've never felt... I've never had so many... Usually, I'm lucky to have one..." She realized she was stammering and wondered why life didn't come with your own personal screenwriter for these difficult conversations. "Never mind."

"Don't stop now." Michael grinned as he left the bed, then bent down and scooped her into his arms. "You're doing wonders for my ego."

"I'm so glad." As if any man who could make a woman feel so spectacular would need help with his ego. "Where are we going?" she asked as he carried her across the living room.

"Back to bed. A dry bed."

"Oh." She hadn't even noticed the bed had gotten wet. "You're a very clever man to have gotten the second bedroom."

"More ego strokes." He laughed, feeling unreasonably lighthearted as he stripped the brocade spread off the queen-size bed. "What a great woman."

This time he laid her on the mattress with more caution than before and for a long, delicious time, they indulged in the slow kisses and tender touches they hadn't taken time for earlier.

"I can't believe how you make me feel," she sighed as his wickedly slow hands made every atom in her body hum.

"How's that?" He pressed his lip to the little heart-shaped birthmark at the base of her spine.

She exhaled a slow rippling sigh of pleasure. "Like I'm floating about three feet above this bed."

"That's a start." He skimmed his tongue up her spine. "Let's see if we can make you fly."

As the night grew longer and the kisses grew deeper, Lorelei discovered that Michael O'Malley was definitely a man of his word.

# 11

LORELEI WAS ROUSED from a light sleep by the insistent ringing of the phone.

"Let me," Michael said, reaching over her as she groped blindly for the bedside telephone. "Just in case... Yeah?"

Amazingly, during the marvelous love-filled night she'd forgotten all about her stalker. Now, reality came crashing down on her again and Lorelei felt every muscle in her body tense as she watched Michael hitch himself up in bed.

"Yeah." He nodded even as he bent his head and brushed a kiss against her tightly set lips. The light kiss assured her that whoever was on the other end of the line didn't represent a problem. "Yeah, I'll tell her." He ran his hand down her back as she snuggled close. "We'll be here another couple of hours. Then I'm moving her someplace else. No point in setting her up as a target if it's not necessary." He hung up the receiver.

"Who was that?"

"Taylor. He called off today's shooting."

"Can he afford to do that?"

"That's not really your problem," Michael replied.

"Don't look a gift day off in the mouth.... Meanwhile," he pulled her on top of him, "where were we?"

Much, much later, they were sitting at the table in the living room. Never much of a breakfast eater, she'd ordered strawberries and cream and a croissant which was flaky and so buttery she feared it undoubtedly had as many calories as the beignets she'd been eating. Strangely, she couldn't seem to care. Michael had a more robust appetite. As she watched him eat his way through an order of eggs sardou, grits and redeye gravy, fried potatoes and thick slabs of tasso, a tangy smoked ham spiced with red pepper, she decided that after the energy he'd used up making love to her all night, he undoubtedly needed the rejuvenating meal.

"Where are we going?" she asked.

"I thought I'd take you to my place. Since it's obvious that whoever is after you is part of the crew, you're a sitting duck staying here."

"Your place?" The scarlet strawberry, nearly as large as a baby's fist, paused on the way to her mouth. "In the bayou?"

"Nah. The cabin's still out there, but it'd be too hard to keep coming back in for filming—"

"So you're not going to argue about that," she murmured. "I was wondering."

"About what?"

"I thought you might try to stop me from finishing the movie."

"I don't like the idea of putting you at risk again," he admitted with a frown. He put down his fork, braced his elbows on the table and linked his fingers together. "But I can understand you feel a commitment to honor your contract."

"Thank you. That's very understanding of you."

"I have my moments."

Although she knew she was venturing into dangerous territory, there was something Lorelei had to know. "What happens after the film wraps?"

He shrugged. "You'll go back to L.A. Get on with your life."

It wasn't what he wanted. It wasn't honestly what he intended. Not really. But Michael didn't figure that this was any time to get into an argument about their future. Besides, he reminded himself, she'd worked hard to establish herself in Hollywood. Why would she consider giving that all up? Even if they were great together—make that world-class—in bed.

Lorelei had been prepared for an argument. She'd even planned a pretty little speech about how she knew that it wasn't going to be easy, juggling her career in Hollywood and his here in New Orleans. But they were intelligent people, she'd planned to say. They could work something out. His casual attitude, after the night they'd shared, stung.

"Are you trying to dump me again?"

"Of course not. I was just saying that— What the hell do you mean, *again?*"

"Well, although I'm not one to hold a grudge, you can't deny that you were the one who wanted to break up in the first place all those years ago."

"Me?" Color rose from his collar. Fire flashed in his

eyes. "You obviously have a rotten memory, sweetheart. Because I wasn't the one who refused to answer all those letters. And who wouldn't come to the phone all Thanksgiving weekend."

A weekend he'd planned to give her a promise ring. The diamond had been merely a chip, but he'd gone without lunches and worked double shifts on the docks for three months while going to college to pay for it. His anger building, Michael stabbed a forkful of golden fried potatoes and shoved them into his mouth to keep from telling her exactly how much her behavior had hurt.

"What letters?"

"Geez." He put the fork down again, took a long drink of chicory coffee, then dragged a hand through his hair. "I might not have written every day like we promised, but I *did* write." Which was more than she'd done. "A lot."

"But, I never..." Her voice drifted off. "It must have been Julie."

"Who's Julie?"

"My roommate in the sorority house. Her mother and mine were Tri-Delts together. They must have cooked up a plan to keep me from getting your letters."

Actually, that suggestion didn't come as all that much of a surprise. It made him angry as hell, but Michael could easily see Maureen Longstreet stooping to such subterfuge.

"You still didn't return my calls when you came home for Thanksgiving vacation."

"I didn't get them," she insisted.

Okay. Since one of her parents, or the housekeeper had answered every time he'd called, until her mother had finally coolly explained that Lorelei didn't want to see him, Michael was willing to buy that, too. However...

"I guess you were too busy with all your sorority sisters, and all your new pals to write to me," he said with far more casualness than he felt. He took another swallow of coffee and wished it were something stronger.

"But I did!"

Her eyes were wide, a white line circled the lush full lips he could still taste, and her hand, as it pressed against her chest, was trembling. Michael had interrogated enough suspects to know when someone was lying. Lorelei was not.

"Aw, hell." He leaned his head against the back of the chair and shut his eyes. The answer, striking like a bolt of lightning from a clear blue sky, was not a pleasant one. "Mom must have ditched them."

"Your mother? But I thought she liked me."

"She did." Michael dragged his hand down his face, then opened his eyes. The hurt expression on her too pale face caused something elemental to move deep inside him. It was at that moment, when he wanted to calm more than he wished to conquer, that Michael knew he was sunk.

"But she never made any secret of the fact that she thought we were too young to be so serious about each other. She was always afraid that you'd get pregnant. And I'd have to drop out of school to support you."

"In order for me to get pregnant, you would have had to have made love to me. Which you constantly refused to do."

Despite the seriousness of the conversation, Michael laughed as he watched her pique overcome her hurt. "I was trying to stay on the straight and narrow for your sake," he insisted. "Hell, if you *had* gotten pregnant, you would have had to give up all your dreams of becoming an actress. If you'd ended up getting married at sixteen, you sure as hell wouldn't be a big star today."

He was undoubtedly right. She probably would have stayed in Louisiana, married Michael and raised a family. And daydreamed about what might have been.

"You never would have forgiven me," he insisted.

Lorelei knew he was right about the possible regrets. Then again, how could she explain that there'd been times over the past years, when she'd think about the family she'd once dreamed of having with Michael, and suffer an entirely different set of regrets.

"We'll never know," she decided reluctantly.

"You're probably right." The buzzer at the door sounded.

"That'll be Shayne. I forgot to call him and tell him that I was going to take the day shift." Michael tossed the damask napkin on the table, stood up and answered the door.

"How are you feeling?" Shayne asked Lorelei as he

sat down at the table and filched a piece of his brother's tasso.

"I'm fine. Really," she insisted when he gave her a long look that could have rivaled his brother's for intimidation tactics.

Despite his easygoing attitude and expensive clothes—he was wearing custom-tailored linen slacks and a cream linen collarless shirt today—Lorelei understood that Shayne O'Malley wasn't the carefree playboy he appeared to be at first glance. In fact, in his own way, she was sure Shayne could be as dangerous as his older brother. Which made her even more interested in meeting the woman capable of holding her own with the former secret agent.

"Good," he said finally. He turned to Michael. "I finished running all those names you gave me through every computer data bank I could hack my way into. Everyone came up as clean as a whistle." He handed the manila envelope to his brother. "I've got something for you, too," he said to Lorelei. "It was waiting downstairs at the desk. I had to open it," he said apologetically.

"I understand." Wondering if this would ever be over, if she'd ever have her privacy back, she opened the envelope. "It's a screenplay," she told Michael, who was watching her carefully. "From Brian." She read the note clipped to the top page. "He says that he knows he'd promised to wait, but since I wasn't going to be doing anything today, he thought I might like to pass the time reading it."

"Interesting he'd assume you wouldn't have anything to do today," Michael drawled.

Although she no longer had any secrets from either of these men, Lorelei felt her cheeks burn. "I think he meant since the shooting was called off," she murmured.

Michael chuckled and Shayne pretended sudden interest in the remaining fried potatoes which he succeeded in polishing off. "Well," he said, pushing back away from the table, "since it seems you have everything under control, Mike, I'm going to dig a little deeper. I left a program running that should be into the mainframe at Bank of America. By the time I get back, I should have a better picture of everyone's cash flow."

"You broke into the crew's bank accounts?" Lorelei asked, appalled at the idea of Michael condoning such a thing. "Isn't that against the law?"

"It's skimming on the edge," Shayne argued. "After what happened to you yesterday, if we had any idea who the guy might be, it's possible the L.A. cops could talk a friendly judge into issuing a search warrant. But we're still working in the dark. And time's running out. Time we don't have."

"Still..." She looked up at Michael, who was standing beside the table, arms folded over his chest. "I have to admit I'm surprised you'd stoop to such an unethical thing."

His jaw firmed, his expression turned as stony as she'd ever seen it. "I'm not going to let anything happen to you, Lorelei."

The idea that this man, whose integrity had always been as unyielding as the Rock of Gibraltar, would go against everything he'd always believed in for her sake stunned her.

"I think I'm beginning to understand why you left the police force."

"Are you suggesting I was a dirty cop?"

Knowing him as well as she did, loving him as she did—and probably always had—Lorelei refused to be intimidated by the steely glare.

"Of course not. But you care, Michael. Sometimes, perhaps, too much."

She thought of what she'd managed to get out of Shayne during their afternoon conversations, how Michael blamed himself for Desiree's nearly being killed because he'd followed police guidelines against his better judgment.

His only answer was a shrug and grunt. But watching him carefully, Lorelei saw the chagrin in his eyes and realized that although he had saved Desiree's life by shooting her attacker, he'd always consider himself responsible for having allowed the man to get so close in the first place.

She considered suggesting that he couldn't save the entire world. Then realized he wouldn't listen. "Desiree was fortunate to have you in her corner," she said simply as she stood up and walked the few steps to where he was standing, statue still. "So am I."

She went up on her toes and kissed him. As their lips clung, Shayne cleared his throat. "Gotta go," he announced. "I'll be at the office if anything comes up."

He let himself out. Neither participant in the lingering kiss heard his pleased, knowing chuckle.

MICHAEL'S HOUSE WAS in the part of New Orleans known as the Faubourg Marigny Historic District. Although it was a little more than a minute's walk from the French Quarter, the distance could have been a hundred years. The neighborhood, which had been established in 1806 as a residential area—the word *faubourg* was French for *suburb*—had originally been settled by French and Spanish Creoles and *des gens des couleurs libres*, or "free persons of color."

Succeeding decades brought immigrants from Italy, Ireland and Germany to the working-class neighborhood. Lorelei recalled from her schooldays that there'd once been so many people of German descent living in the little wedge of land between Esplanade and Elysian Fields that for a time the neighborhood had been known as Little Saxony.

"This must be convenient to your office," she said as he drove past worn frame and brick buildings now housing jazz clubs and restaurants.

"It is. But that's not why I chose it."

"Why did you?" She was surprised by the revitalization of the neighborhood that had been going downhill when she'd left the city. "When the Quarter's even closer."

"The Quarter's changed a lot since you left," he said. "In a scramble for tourist dollars, it's turned into the Theme Park from Hell. In fact, when you get right down to it, even the lofty environs of your parents'

Garden District now has tour buses clogging the streets and fouling the air. The way I see it, this neighborhood is one of the last remaining antidotes to the town's chronic case of the cutes."

Thinking about the way the landmark Jax Brewery had been turned into a glitzy shopping mall, and how the ubiquitous tacky souvenir T-shirt shops seemed to have sprung up like weeds, Lorelei decided he had a point.

"Besides, I like the pace here," he said as he turned off Frenchmen Avenue and pulled into a crumbling brick driveway. "People still walk instead of drive, and although things admittedly get a little juiced up outside the clubs after the sun goes down, during the day there are two speeds—Stop and Mildew."

She laughed appreciatively. Laughter that died off as she studied the house he'd parked beside. "This is yours?"

"It mostly belongs to the bank. But they let me live here." He cut the engine and pocketed the key.

"It's darling." The quaint, Easter egg bright five-sided cottage had been built to conform to the quirky wedge-shaped lot. Such lots were not uncommon in the neighborhoods outside the original French Quarter grid since engineers had been forced to adjust their street schemes to the winding curves of the nearby river.

The house, set French-style against the banquette, or sidewalk, and constructed of stuccoed brick, had been painted in traditional Creole colors of putty, French red, and Egyptian blue.

"I'm still in the processing of remodeling," Michael apologized as he unlocked the narrow wooden hurricane doors covering the entrance to the historic cottage. "I figure, what with all the work that needs to be done, and my budget, it's undoubtedly a lifetime project."

"A labor of love," she murmured, taking in the interior living room wall that revealed the pink handmade bricks. The ceiling featured wonderful hand-cut beaded cypress ceiling beams. It crossed Lorelei's mind that her mother, who'd never been a fan of Michael O'Malley, would definitely approve of his home.

He shrugged. "That's on the good days. There are times when I think I must have gone mad the day I cashed out my pension plan to buy it."

"It's probably a better investment than the usual IRA." She edged past the sawhorses holding a plank oak door he'd obviously been sanding and went through an arched doorway that led to the back of the house.

"The courtyard was one of the reasons I bought the place," he said at her sharp intake of breath.

"I'd be tempted, too." Her appreciative gaze drank in the triangle-shaped space filled with lush green subtropical plants. Although they appeared to be growing wildly, the mood—enhanced by a bubbling fountain and redbrick patio shaded by the leafy, spreading black limbs of an oak that had to be nearly three hundred years old—was that of a calming oasis. "It's like a secret garden."

Lorelei had grown up in this city renowned for its hidden courtyards. This, she decided, was one of the most magnificent she'd ever seen.

"I'm glad you like it," Michael mumbled, feeling suddenly like a tongue-tied teenager again. It shouldn't matter so much that she like the house he'd fallen in love with at first sight. He shouldn't even care what she thought.

But he did, dammit.

"I adore it."

Accepting his offer of a tour, Lorelei oohed and aahed as they moved from room to room. The octagon-shaped room that shared an interior door with the master bedroom, which he was currently using as a study, would be perfect for a nursery, she thought idly. When the unconscious thought struck home, Lorelei realized that the idea of raising Michael's babies in this darling Creole cottage was more than a little appealing.

As she ran her fingers over the hand-carved headboard of the yellow pine poster bed he'd been born in and that his mother had given him the day he'd closed on the house, Michael found himself envisioning making love to Lorelei in this bed. Imagined her giving birth to their own sons and daughters, pictured a lifetime of lazy Sunday breakfasts in bed.

Such thoughts, Michael decided, were not only dangerous, they were definitely premature. Right now his responsibility was to keep Lorelei safe. His mind needed to be sharp and clear, which meant he couldn't allow himself to indulge in romantic fantasies. No matter how pleasing.

"You'd probably like to read that script Wilder sent over," he said. He'd watched her sneaking peeks at it on the short drive from the hotel.

"If you wouldn't mind. Although I'd planned to take some time off after this film, Brian will undoubtedly keep asking me if I've looked at it."

"Wouldn't want to disappoint the guy," Michael agreed dryly. For some reason he didn't like the screenwriter and although that alone would have given him reason to suspect the guy, Michael couldn't ignore the fact that he was jealous of Wilder's easy friendship with Lorelei, not to mention his aristocratic blond good looks, which he figured any woman would find appealing.

"If you'd rather I didn't—"

"No." Now he was being petty, which wasn't at all like him. What the hell was Lorelei doing to his mind? "Go ahead. I've got some reports I should finish up, anyway."

"If you're sure."

Her eagerness to please made him feel guilty. He smiled reassuringly. "Positive."

They spent the next hour in the courtyard. Michael heard Lorelei sigh as she finished reading the screenplay.

He glanced up from his paperwork. "Not up to his usual standard?"

"Oh, it's good." She traced the title with her fingernail, as if trying to choose her words carefully. "Actually, it's very good. But I think perhaps we've made too many movies together. He seems to be getting in a rut."

"I see," Michael said, not really seeing anything at all.

"It's another woman-in-jeopardy script. Set here in New Orleans."

Although he understood her concern about being typecast, Michael liked the idea of her work bringing her back to the city. "I read in a New Orleans magazine that we're becoming a hot locale for films."

"True. But this one's so dark." She frowned down at the computer-printed pages. "And after what I've been going through, the idea of being held captive in some former slave quarters is not exactly my idea of a fun flick."

"I can see why you might be hesitant to agree to the part," Michael said carefully. He felt as if he were out in the bayou, treading on unstable ground.

He wanted to simply tell her that she belonged here in New Orleans with him, that somehow they could work out their schedules to allow a life together. But then he remembered other women—Desiree in particular—chiding him for possessing an overabundance of male chauvinism. He was hesitant to begin offering advice for fear Lorelei might think he was pressuring her.

Trying to become a modern man of the nineties sure as hell wasn't easy, Michael considered blackly.

Lorelei watched his expression darken and won-

dered at the cause. She'd thought she'd convinced him
that she and Brian were merely friends.

"There's another problem." She gave another soft
sigh. "I'm afraid he'll take it personally if I turn it
down. It's obvious that he wasn't kidding when he
said he wrote this screenplay with me in mind."

"It fits you that well?" Modern male or not, Michael
didn't like the idea of any other man knowing Lorelei's inner thoughts and feelings.

"Actually, she's more of a victim than I would be,"
Lorelei said. "And a lot more innocent. But he kept
making a strange mistake. He kept typing my name
instead of the character's."

Michael felt the hairs at the back of his neck stand
up in a way he'd learned to trust. "Can I read it?" he
asked mildly, not wanting to upset her unnecessarily.
After all, so long as she was with him, she'd be safe.

She smiled, obviously pleased that he'd want to
share her work. "Of course." She handed it over.
"Meanwhile, if you don't mind me borrowing your
bed, I think I'll take a nap. For some reason—" her
eyes sparkled with humor "—I didn't get much sleep
last night."

"You're welcome to anything I've got. Including my
bed." He glanced down at the screenplay he was holding, torn between conflicting needs. "Want some company?"

"The offer's more than a little tempting. But I don't
think I'd get any sleep."

He studied the pale purple shadows beneath her remarkable eyes. "Why don't we compromise?" he sug-

gested. "You get some rest, I'll read the script and then—" he waggled his eyebrows in a theatrically seductive way that made her laugh "—I'll come wake you up."

Her smile could have lit up the entire city of New Orleans for months. She stood up, plunked herself down on his lap, cuddled close and kissed him. A long, sweet kiss that made Michael's head swim with hunger and desire coil in his gut.

He ran his hand down her hair then played with the pale ends that were brushing the tips of her breasts. Tips that tightened to the hardness of rubies beneath his touch. "Maybe I'll read the script later."

She laughed again, marveling that she could feel so carefree after what had happened yesterday, linked her fingers with his and lifted their joined hands to her smiling mouth. "Read the script now." She brushed her lips over his knuckles. "After last night, I need to recoup my strength."

He loved looking at her. Loved touching her. Loved just sitting around with her. Hell, Michael realized suddenly, he just plain loved her. The thought, which once would have been enough to strike terror in his bachelor's heart was eminently satisfying.

"Are you saying you can't keep up with me?"

She trailed her free hand down his chest, toying with his buttons as her expression changed before his eyes. She was no longer Lorelei, the young girl he'd loved and lost. Nor was she the woman he'd come to love again. She'd suddenly become every dangerous femme fatale in every movie he'd ever seen—Bette

Davis in *Jezebel*, Vivien Leigh's Scarlett O'Hara, Kim Novak's enigmatic siren in *Vertigo*, Lorelei's sexy cat burglar in *Hot Ice*. Michael stared, transfixed at the metamorphosis.

"Believe me, darling," she purred, nipping playfully at his earlobe, "the question is not whether I can keep up with you. But whether—and how long—you can keep up with me."

Looking at her, Michael feared that just might be true. "Never let it be said that Michael O'Malley backed down from a challenge."

Lorelei's answering laugh was at first low and sultry, then slipped into silvery delight as she fell out of her siren character. "I love you, Michael O'Malley." Before he could respond, she pressed her fingers against his lips.

"No," she said quickly, "you don't have to say anything, Michael. Not now. I understand that you're a man accustomed to thinking things through, and this has all happened so fast. I also realize that you're undoubtedly going to point out that danger is a potent aphrodisiac, but that truly isn't responsible for the way I feel.

"I *do* love you," she insisted. "Maybe I never stopped loving you. But I'm willing to wait until you're sure about your feelings for me."

That said, she gave him another quick, heartfelt kiss, then ran from the courtyard, leaving him alone. Michael considered going after her. But as he caught sight of the bound screenplay she'd left on the table, responsibility reared its head. He'd check it out, he de-

cided. Then there'd be plenty of time to tell Lorelei
how he felt, all night to show her how much he loved
her, too.

# 12

LESS THAN TEN MINUTES after Lorelei had fled the garden, the phone rang. Michael picked up the cordless extension he'd taken outside with him on the second ring.

"Yeah?"

"Hey, Mike, how're things going?"

"You wouldn't believe it if I told you." Then Michael thought about the way Shayne looked whenever Bliss was in the room, the way he mooned about her whenever she went out of town on her antique buying trips and decided that his brother probably would understand.

"Actually, I might surprise you," Shayne said cheerfully, unknowingly seconding his brother's opinion. "And I hate to be the one to break up your stolen day with Lorelei, but there's a storm front coming in tonight that could bring a lot of wind and rain."

"So?"

"So Taylor decided he couldn't skip work today after all. The shooting's back on schedule."

"Hell." Michael glared down at the pages he'd read so far. Lorelei was right. The script was too close to real life for comfort. He'd wanted to make a few calls. To check things out.

"No problem," Shayne said when Michael told him his problem. "I can take her to the warehouse. After all, I'm supposed to be handling days anyway."

It was, Michael thought, a practical solution. But...

"I'll take good care of her, Mike," Shayne said, displaying an uncanny ability to read his brother's mind. "I'll watch her the same way I would Bliss under the circumstances."

It was, Michael admitted, all that he could ask. Besides, Shayne wasn't exactly an amateur. Although he hadn't shared a great deal about what he'd been doing the past decade, Michael knew that during his years working as a secret agent, or spy, or whatever the hell his brother had been, Shayne had certainly survived more than his share of dangerous situations.

"I worry about her," he admitted.

"I know. That's the down side of love," Shayne said. "But all the good stuff makes it worthwhile."

Remembering how Bliss had almost been killed not so long ago, Michael knew that his brother did understand. All too well.

"You're not a bad kid," he drawled. "For a baby brother."

"And you're not so bad, either. For a big brother," Shayne said with a laugh. "I'll be over in about ten minutes."

Ten minutes, Michael thought as he hung up the phone. He considered waking Lorelei up and making quick furious love to her, but as much as he wanted her again, the idea of Shayne walking in on them was not an appealing one.

"Later," he promised himself as he entered the bedroom and was struck by the provocative sight of her lying on her stomach in his bed. Hell. She looked even better than in his fantasies.

"Later," he repeated fifteen minutes later as he kissed her goodbye.

"Later," she agreed.

And then she was gone. Michael looked up at the sky, viewed the thick pewter clouds rolling in from the Gulf, and damned the weather system that had screwed up his romantic plans for the day.

By the time he'd skimmed through the rest of the screenplay, Michael was even more worried. He drove the few blocks to his office, where the computer Shayne had installed had begun kicking out reams of paper that gave him an intimate look at the finances of all the crew members who'd come to New Orleans for the location shoot.

Knowing Nelson's gambling problems, Michael wasn't surprised that the cameraman didn't have any savings accounts or that his credit cards were all in default. Other than a paid off five-year-old Mustang, Dennis the prop guy had no credit history. Taylor seemed to spend money like it was water. Then again, Michael decided with a mental shrug, the director obviously had it to spend.

He skimmed through the pages listing the checks Wilder had written over the past three months.

"Interesting," Michael murmured as one particular item caught his eye. He'd just reached for the phone to call a local real estate office when he heard the jangle of the bell on the downstairs door.

Since it was Monday, the day Bliss closed the shop, and since he knew from Shayne that she would be in Houma at an estate sale until late afternoon, Michael tensed. Then he pulled the gun from his shoulder holster, slowly opened his office door and began creeping down the stairs.

SHAYNE PARKED OUTSIDE the building where today's filming was to take place. The warehouse had been rented for the week. Michael had checked the place out two days earlier, and although he'd professed concern that there were too many blind corners, they'd both agreed that as long as they didn't let Lorelei out of their sight, it should be okay.

After last night's so-called accident, Shayne didn't feel nearly as sanguine about the location as he had earlier.

He opened the door with the key Taylor had messengered over to his office, and led the way down an aisle between stacks of boxes and crates. "Hey," he called out, "where is everyone?"

When the only answer was the echo of his own voice in the cavernous building, he realized they'd been set up.

"What's wrong?" Lorelei asked, her eyes widening as he pulled the pistol from the back of his linen slacks.

"Don't ask any questions," he said under his breath. "We're going to leave the way we came in. And if anything happens to me, I want you to run like hell and call Michael from the car phone. Whatever you do," he stressed, "don't stop to look back."

"I don't understand. Where is everyone?" Comprehension came crashing down on her as the unmistakable retort of a gunshot rang out. She heard Shayne's vicious curse, watched him stumble, saw the blood spurting out of his shoulder. "Oh, no." She dropped to her knees beside him.

"I told you, dammit, get out of here." Shayne's words were slurred, his voice sounded as if it were coming from a very long way away. "It's not safe."

"I can't leave you." Heedless of the blood, she put her hands beneath his armpits and began dragging him along the concrete floor.

"Go," he insisted, with the dazed look of pain in his eyes. "Call Michael...he needs to know..."

"It's okay," she assured him, ducking as another shot from somewhere up above them whizzed past her ear. "It'll be all right, Shayne.... It's only a few more feet to the door...."

Shayne, who'd fallen unconscious, couldn't hear her. Limp as he was, he seemed to weigh a ton; her heart was pounding and her breathing grew labored as she struggled to get this man who'd become like a brother to her to safety.

She was less than six feet from the door when a man jumped down from a tower of crates in front of her. "What's the hurry, sweetheart?"

Lorelei stared at the man she'd thought was her friend. "Oh, please, don't let it be you!"

"Sorry." Brian Wilder's grin was as dashing as ever. But there was a maniacal look in his eyes that terrified her. "You were expecting Eric, perhaps? Or John? Or Dennis?"

"Despite what Michael said, I honestly didn't suspect any of you." At her feet, Shayne groaned. To her horror, the screenwriter aimed the gun at the unconscious man's chest. "Please, Brian," she implored, "I'll do whatever you want. Go wherever you please. Just don't hurt Shayne any more."

"You don't understand." His smile was that same horrible friendly one that was at such odds with his murderous behavior. "You're going to go wherever I want, anyway, Lorelei. And do whatever I want. You have no choice, you see. But I can't afford to leave witnesses."

Lorelei heard a bloodcurdling scream as he pulled the trigger and realized it had been torn from her own throat. Then, remembering what Shayne had wanted her to do, she fled the warehouse.

Brian, who'd been on the verge of ensuring that the detective was dead, cursed as he realized she'd taken off.

"Bitch!" he roared. Then, having no choice but to abandon the man he'd just shot point-blank through the chest, he began running after her.

Lorelei had almost reached the car when he caught up with her. Grabbing hold of her flowing silver hair, he yanked her off her feet, making her fall. Lorelei felt her head slam against the blacktop. Then everything went dark.

MICHAEL CAME AROUND the corner of a display of stuffed teddy bears and found himself aiming his gun at a man who could have been a mirror image of himself. In twenty year's time.

"What the hell?" He stared at his father in disbelief. His tone was not the slightest bit welcoming.

"What's the matter, Michael?" Patrick O'Malley asked casually, as if it hadn't been fifteen years since the last time he'd visited his son. "Don't you recognize your own father?"

Michael cursed and put the pistol away. "I could have shot you." The situation was too much like the recent one with Shayne and he hated knowing that his father—whose photographer's eyes never missed a thing—could see his hands shake.

"I imagine there have been times when you'd have been glad to do precisely that," Patrick agreed.

Michael didn't answer. There was no need. "What are you doing here?"

"Didn't Roarke tell you?"

"Tell me what?"

"I called him last month to assure him I'd be home for his wedding."

"He probably didn't mention it because he figured you'd miss it. Like you did all his birthdays."

"Actually, I was there for his sixth," Patrick argued. "I remember because it was a bitch getting a flight out of the Sudan. And I made his eleventh."

"It was his twelfth. And you were a week late."

Patrick shrugged shoulders as wide as Michael's own. "Close enough."

Even if he hadn't been worried about Lorelei, Michael wouldn't have been in the mood for reminiscing with the man who'd abandoned his family, leaving his eldest son to take over the role of man of the house.

"Look, Dad, I'm sure Roarke's going to be tickled pink that you showed up." Actually, Michael wasn't certain about that at all. Although the middle O'Malley brother might not dislike their father with the intensity Michael did, he'd never exactly been a fan of the guy, either. "But right now I've got work to do, and—"

He cursed as the phone in his office started ringing. Turning his back on his father, he took the stairs two at a time. "Blue Bayou Investigations," he managed to answer on the third ring. "Yeah, Dirkson," he said as his former partner at the NOPD identified himself. "What's up?"

Michael felt all the blood leave his face. "I'll be right there." He slammed the receiver down and took off running.

"What's happened?" Patrick, who'd followed him into the office shouted as he ran after his son.

"Shayne's been shot. They took him to Tulane. And Lorelei's missing."

"Shayne's shot? How is he? He isn't—"

"I don't know, dammit."

Michael's hands were trembling as he tried to unlock his car door. It took three attempts before he managed to get the key into the lock and by then his father had caught up with him. He didn't want to deal with old childhood hurts while his heart was ripping apart.

He didn't want to have anything to do with this man who'd made his mother cry for so many years.

But unable to leave his father alone on the sidewalk after having just informed him that the son he'd never bothered to get to know was lying in a hospital, possibly dead, Michael threw himself into the driver's seat and reached across to unlock the passenger door. He gunned the engine, peeling rubber as he roared away from the curb before Patrick could get his seat belt fastened.

"Lorelei?" Patrick asked as they tore through the streets at a speed that didn't even approach the legal limit. "Is that the little Longstreet girl you had a thing for?"

Michael shot him a look. "How do you know about that?"

"Your mother told me all about it in her letters. Including how she'd kept you from receiving the letters the girl sent from college. I never approved of that," Patrick divulged.

It was one more stunner in a day that had already had more than its share of shocks. "Mom wrote to you?"

"Nearly every other month."

"For all these years?"

"Of course."

"Of course." Michael shook his head. "I don't imagine you wrote back."

"Whenever I could."

Michael cursed as he looked up into the rearview mirror and saw flashing lights behind him. He had two choices. He could make a run for it. Or he could pull over and talk his way out of the ticket, which after all his years on the force, he had no doubt he could do.

Not wanting to get involved in a potentially deadly police chase, he pulled over, leaped out of the car and headed back to the patrol car. Fortunately, the cop recognized him immediately, Michael explained the problem and was promptly on his way again, this time with a police escort.

"I'm impressed," Patrick murmured. "But not surprised. Your mother told me that you were well thought of in the department."

"Mom seems to have been a font of information all these years," Michael said through clenched teeth.

"Since you've never been married yourself, I don't think you're in any position to judge any other couple's relationship," Patrick said mildly. "I love your mother, in my own way. She always understood that."

Michael's response, as he pulled up outside the emergency room doors of Tulane Medical Center, was another rough curse.

LORELEI AWOKE to find herself on a bed in a room that at first seemed as dark as the inside of a tomb. As her eyes gradually adjusted to the lack of light, she realized that a kerosene lantern set atop a heavy stone pillar was making flickering shadows on the brick walls. Shadows that resembled demons dancing. Her head was pounding. Her arms, most particularly her wrists, ached. She tried to rub her aching temple, heard a metallic jangle and belatedly realized she'd been chained to the wall behind the bed.

"I wouldn't do that if I were you," a calm, all-too-familiar voice offered. The rusty bedsprings creaked as Brian sat on the edge of the bare mattress. "You'll only succeed in bruising your wrists even more."

Although his tone was mild, his eyes were not. In the stuttering lantern light Lorelei saw the fever and the madness.

She forced her whirling, pain-fogged mind to concentrate on what was most important: getting out of this horrendous situation alive. Of course he'd never be able to get away with this. The trick was to make sure she was still alive when Michael arrived to rescue her.

"Where are we?" she asked. The windows were covered with heavy wooden shutters. Lorelei had no idea how long she'd been unconscious, no clue as to whether it was night or day.

"My secret place." He smiled down at her.

"That's not very illuminating."

"It's not important for you to know. Since you're not going to be leaving here."

She'd been afraid of that. Tamping down her icy terror, she managed to soften her expression. Her eyes became wide and guileless.

"I'm a woman," she murmured, just a little bit coyly. "You know how curious we are."

He smiled at that. "I also know what a slut you are."

The word, calmly spoken, was like a stone striking

her heart. "Brian, you're mistaken. If you'd just unfasten me, we could talk about this and—"

"No." He hit her with the back of his hand. Hard. Another slap to her other cheek made her face burn. "I'm not stupid, Lorelei. There's no way I'm going to let you talk your way out of the punishment you deserve." He frowned as he reached out a fingertip and traced the cut his gold-and-agate signet ring had made on her cheekbone.

"I didn't plan for it to be this way," he murmured, as much to himself as to her. "When I found this plantation house while researching locations for my screenplay, I envisioned us living here together.

"I was going to worship you, as I've always done. I was going to initiate you into the wonders of love.... I knew, since you were so innocent, that you'd be frightened—"

"I am," she admitted, jumping on the idea that if he'd taken her to a plantation house, they must be somewhere out along the river. Or, perhaps in the bayou. That was not an encouraging thought. There were miles of swampland surrounding New Orleans. How would Michael ever find her in time?

He couldn't, Lorelei decided. Which meant she was on her own. Suddenly a horrifying memory swam into focus.

"You shot Shayne." Tears stung her eyes. Grief was a fist twisting her heart.

"He deserved to die. After what he'd done with you."

"He never did anything. Except be a friend."

"That's my point." Brian's laugh was dry and lacked humor. "The bastard was entirely too friendly, if you get my drift." He leered at her as he ran his hand over her supine body. The slow, threatening caress made her tremble.

"Do you want me?" he asked idly, as his fingers painfully closed over her breast. "Or are you shivering because you're afraid of me?"

Lorelei prayed she could pull off the most important role in her life. "I think both," she murmured, allowing her fear to remain in her eyes as she struggled to portray unwilling desire as well. "I'm afraid you're going to hurt me—"

"Oh, I am." When his wicked fingers moved to her other breast, she bit her lip rather than cry out.

"But I'm also afraid I'm going to like it," she said, forcing herself to look right into those eyes where madness swirled.

It was obvious that the lie—the biggest, baldest one she'd ever told in her life—caught him by surprise. He studied her for what seemed an eternity.

"You've been screwing that detective. O'Malley."

She thought about denying it, remembered the camera that had been installed in her bedroom in Malibu and feared that perhaps Brian had proof of his accusation. Although she hated the idea that he might have watched her making love with Michael, she managed, just barely, to keep the distaste from her expression.

"It didn't mean anything." She tried to shrug, but was prevented by the way her arms had been pulled so tightly above her head. "I thought, perhaps if I allowed Michael to make love to me, it would get my mind off the man I really wanted." She paused, slowly licking her dry lips as she managed to hold his gaze. "It didn't."

"Are you talking about me?"

Lorelei thought he suddenly seemed unsure of himself. And, perhaps, a bit hopeful. Remembering how the first letters had professed undying devotion—the veiled threats had come later—she tried to coax Brian back to that initial emotional mind-set.

"The chemistry has always been there between us, Brian. If we didn't feel it, we couldn't work so well together. If you didn't understand me so well, you could never write such marvelous scripts for me."

"I did, you know. Write them just for you." His hand moved down her torso, following the curve of her waist, the flare of her hip. "No one else."

"I know." His touch was making her skin crawl. In the early days of her career, Lorelei had played a woman trapped in a well, covered with cockroaches. The experience had been horrifying, but at that moment if she'd had a choice between cockroaches and Brian's hands, she would have taken the roaches.

Keep him talking, she reminded herself. It's your only chance.

His fingers tightened on her thigh, digging into her skin in a way she knew would leave bruises.

"I thought you were pure."

Bruises would fade, Lorelei reminded herself. Unfortunately, death was permanent. "I realize that now." She managed, just barely, to make her tone both apologetic and conciliatory. "I also realize that I betrayed you. Betrayed our relationship. But the truth is, Brian, I never realized how you felt about me....

"I mean, I knew that *I* loved *you*. I dreamed about you, fantasized about you. But you never said anything. How was I to know that you felt the same way?"

It was, she thought, a good point. A logical point. Unfortunately, there was nothing logical about either this man or her situation.

"You should have read my mind," he scolded. "The way I can read yours."

"Perhaps I'm not as clever as you. Or as intuitive. You're the writer, Brian. Creating characters and stories must take a great deal of imagination and intuition. I'm merely the actress, reciting the wonderful words you've written."

She was laying it on with a trowel, she knew and groaned inwardly, certain that she'd gone too far with such false flattery. Fortunately, Brian seemed to grow in stature at the idea of her merely being a piece of malleable clay for him to mold as he liked.

"I suppose you have a point," he murmured. He leaned forward and ran his hand down her cheek. "Perhaps I've misunderstood the situation."

Before she could assure him that he had, and implore him to unfasten her restraints so she could show him how much she cared for him, a sound suddenly shattered the silence.

"A boat!" He jumped up, went over to the window, and flung open the shutters. The predicted storm was almost upon them, coloring the evening air a strange, eerie hue of yellow; Lorelei saw a sulfurous flash of lighting on the horizon.

"It's probably just a fisherman," she said reassuringly. Damn. He was tense again, nervousness radiating from every pore like a deadly aura.

"Or it could be O'Malley." He slammed the shutters closed and took the gun—the same gun he'd used to shoot Shayne, Lorelei realized—from his belt. "One brother down." He actually laughed. "One more to go."

He paused in the doorway. "I'll be back."

Under any other conditions, it could have been a promise. But as she heard his footfalls clattering on the wooden stairs, Lorelei knew his words were a deadly threat.

"Damn!" She yanked against the chains with all her might, determined to take advantage of Brian's absence to free herself. Although the abrupt gesture caused the metal of the handcuffs to dig even more deeply into her wrists, Lorelei considered the abrasions a small price to pay for freedom.

She thought she felt the left hand give. Just a little. More determined, she tugged harder, closing her eyes and gritting her teeth, putting her entire body into the effort. Finally, she was rewarded when the mortar surrounding one of the bricks crumbled and she was able to pull her hand free. She twisted around, got up on her knees, and used the spike that had been imbedded in the wall as a chisel.

The effort was not silent. As she banged the iron

spike against the stone wall, digging out the two-hundred-year-old mortar, Lorelei feared that Brian would be able to hear her all the way downstairs.

But it didn't really matter, because he had every intention of killing her. If she was going to die, at least this way she'd die fighting for her life.

THERE WERE NO WORDS for how Michael felt when he burst into the emergency room and found his brother sitting up on a metal gurney, grimacing as a nurse swabbed antiseptic over the torn flesh of his shoulder. Relief didn't even come close.

"I thought you were dead."

"There was a moment I thought so, too," Shayne said grimly, cursing beneath his breath as the nurse hit a particularly sensitive spot. "He obviously nicked an artery when he got off that first shot. My shoulder started bleeding like a stuck pig. But thank God for Kevlar body vests."

"Yeah." Michael looked at the ugly, darkening bruise on Shayne's chest, just over his heart, and realized how close he'd come to losing his brother.

"Mike, I feel horrible about Lorelei."

"We'll find her." Michael could not allow himself to think otherwise."

"If I'd only been more careful. If I'd only checked out the warehouse myself, first—"

"Don't second-guess yourself. If you'd gone in first, you would have had to leave her in the car. You had no idea you were being set up, Shayne. Hell, I'm the one who let her go in the first place. If anything happens to her, it'll be my fault."

"I'm the one who took the case," Shayne argued.

"You boys are wasting time," Patrick, who'd managed to smooth-talk the dragon guarding the ER into letting him into the treatment room, said. "One thing I've learned is once a thing is done, there's no looking back. You've got to move on. And find that little girl."

"Pop?" Shayne looked at his brother. "What the hell is he doing here?"

"It's a long story. And one I don't have time for. I've got to call Roarke."

"Tell him I've come home for his nuptials," Patrick instructed.

"I'll leave that bit of news for you to tell him," Michael replied over his shoulder as he left the room.

Five minutes later, he'd learned the name of the real estate agent who'd sold Brian Wilder the crumbling plantation along the Great River Road and gotten the location of the house. Then he arranged to have Daria Shea, Roarke's fiancée, go to the shop to wait for Bliss's return, in case Bliss heard the news about Shayne being shot on the news. He also placed a call to the parish sheriff, asking that he get as many men as he could—including a SWAT team—to the plantation as soon as possible.

Roarke agreed to call their mother, tell her about Shayne, and assure her that her youngest son would survive with nothing more than a sore shoulder and bruised ribs. Michael thought about having Roarke warn their mother about Patrick's return, but since she hadn't let her sons in on the little fact that she'd kept in touch with her husband all these years, he decided to stay out of the marriage he'd never been able to understand.

Leaving Shayne to deal with the immediate problem of their father, Michael left the hospital and headed for the river. And Lorelei.

LORELEI TENSED as she heard Brian's roar. "It's the damn sheriff!" Her spirits soared when, at that same moment, she managed to pull herself loose.

Which was only the first step, she reminded herself, swallowing the desire to shout out her victory. She still had to figure out a way to get out of the house. Away from Brian.

Although the shutters were closed, she could hear the *tap tap tap* of the rain on the roof. The howl of the wind blowing over the river sounded like the lonely wail of lost souls. She opened the shutters, discouraged to see that even if she did manage to break out the glass, she was at least three stories above the marshy ground.

There was no way she could escape by jumping. She'd have to try to slip down the stairs. Then find her way to the door, without getting shot. Like Shayne.

Tears flooded her eyes as she remembered Michael's brother lying in that pool of blood on the concrete floor. So much blood. And Brian had shot him again, in the chest, at such close range.... How could he have possibly survived?

Swiping at the tears that had begun to stream down

her cheeks, she blinked furiously, reminding herself that there would be time to grieve for Shayne after she'd escaped. He'd given his life for her. She owed it to him to make such a valiant sacrifice worthwhile.

She considered calling out to the men on the boat that was coming into view, but was afraid that they'd never be able to hear her over the sound of the motor and the roar of the wind. Perhaps she could wave the lantern....

She'd turned away from the window when a gunshot rang out from inside the house. A moment later, answering shots came from the river. She held her breath, wondering if they'd killed Brian. Unfortunately, the sound of his boots pounding on the stairs told her otherwise.

He stopped in the open doorway, his eyes looking like burning coals in the ashen hue of his complexion. "What the hell are you doing?"

He was still holding the gun. Lorelei tensed, waiting for the explosion, the inevitable pain. But instead of shooting, he lunged at her, giving her a chance to dodge out of the way. Just barely.

His fingers grabbed hold of her blouse. Over his curses and her screams, the sound of fabric ripping was barely noticeable. She pulled free again and swung her right arm, catching him across the face with the heavy chain that was still attached to the handcuff locked around her wrist.

There was the sound of bone breaking. It was his turn to scream as blood began pouring from his nose. Taking advantage of the distraction, Lorelei tore out of the room, headed for the stairs. She heard him stumbling after her, heard the crash of the stone pillar he tipped over in his pain and haste, heard the footfalls just behind her on the stairs.

She had just reached the first landing, when there was another sound. A sudden swoosh. Then a blinding flash. Lorelei couldn't resist looking back. The kerosene must have spilled from the lantern when he'd knocked over the pillar. The aged and rotted wood had gone up like dry tinder.

Flames were roaring down the stairs behind her. Just ahead of them she could see Brian, his face covered with blood.

She kept running. Faster. She tripped over the chain dangling from her wrist and was suddenly tumbling, terrifyingly out of control, head over heels, until coming to an abrupt stop on another landing. As she pushed herself to her feet again, ignoring the pain shooting up her ankle, Lorelei realized that the frightening fall had gotten her downstairs faster than she could have run. For the first time, Brian was no longer in sight.

With her heart pounding deafeningly in her ears, she clattered down the last ten steps, and cried with relief when she discovered the stairs ended only a few feet from the front door. She raced across the rotten mahogany floorboards, refusing to obey Brian's shouted instructions to stop, scarcely noticing the bullet that whizzed past her head and imbedded itself in the door frame.

She reached for the handle. One more second, she assured herself. Then she'd be free.

DRIVING LIKE A MANIAC, Michael arrived minutes after the sheriff. The sight of the flames shooting out of the windows was not an encouraging one.

"The guy's already shot at us once," the lawman informed him. "Then he disappeared inside the house. A couple minutes later, we saw the flames. Then heard another shot."

"From inside?"

"Yeah."

Michael refused to allow himself to believe that he was too late. He knew he'd never forgive himself if Wilder had killed Lorelei.

"I'm going in."

The sheriff caught his arm. "You can't do that."

"The place is nothing but dry rot. It's a tinderbox. There's no way I'm leaving her in there to be burned to death."

"You might have been a hotshot cop, O'Malley," the sheriff argued, "but this here is my jurisdiction. And I'm saying that I want you to get behind the damn police line."

"I'm going in there, Sheriff." Michael pulled out his gun. "And the only way you're going to stop me is to have your men shoot me in the back."

That said, he started running toward the house.

"Hold your fire," the sheriff called out to his men, his voice thick with disgust. And frustration.

Opting for speed over caution, Michael threw himself against the heavy oak front door just as Lorelei reached for it. The wood slammed against her, knocking her to the floor, but before she could realize what was happening, Michael had scooped her up and was carrying her out of the house even as another bullet crashed into the door frame.

The rain was pelting down on them like stinging needles as he carried her to safety. Thunder rolled like caisson fire; lightning lit up the sky.

"Michael?" She couldn't believe he'd come. Then again, another part of her knew that she'd always believed he would.

"It's okay." Only a minute ago, he'd wanted to kill Wilder for what the son of a bitch had done to two of the people he cared most about in the world. Two people he loved. Now, as he held Lorelei close, and buried his face in her wet hair, Michael could only thank God that she was alive.

"It's okay." He said the words over and over again, like a mantra. "You're okay." He kissed her face and tasted both tears and rain.

She was trembling like a willow in a Gulf Coast hurricane.

"But Shayne—"

"Is okay, too."

Surely that was impossible! "But I saw him—"

"He was wearing a bulletproof vest. And the shoulder wound isn't as bad as it looked."

"Oh, thank God!"

Lorelei clung to him, laughing and crying all at the same time. There was another stuttering flash of lightning and then she saw Brian engulfed in flames like some villain from a horror movie, stagger out the door, the gun still in his hand.

Amazingly, even as he was about to die, the screenwriter she'd once thought was her friend, raised the gun as if to shoot. The reckless gesture earned a barrage of bullets from the members of the SWAT team.

"It's over," Michael promised her, holding her close, pressing her face against his chest to keep her from having to look at the dead man.

As horrifying as the events of this day she knew she'd never forget had been, Lorelei felt her terror giving way to a much deeper emotion.

She tilted her head back and looked up at him. "I hate to argue with the knight in shining armor who just saved my life a second time in as many days, but you're wrong, Michael." Her smile was wobbly, but warmed with the love that was echoed in her tear-brightened eyes. "It's just beginning."

# _____Epilogue_____

IT WAS A HOT steamy day in the bayou. But none of the guests assembled for the wedding were complaining. The myriad members of his mother's family—the strong Cajun branch of Michael's family tree—had outdone themselves preparing a feast of spicy shrimp gumbo, jambalaya, crayfish, blackened catfish and grilled fillet of alligator with a tabasco sauce guaranteed to clear the sinuses.

Marsh gas glowed a phosphorous green as the sun settled into the water; sparks flew upward from the Broussard clan's barbecues; fireflies flickered among the Spanish moss-draped branches of ancient Cypress trees, seeming almost to dance in time to the jaunty zydeco Michael's cousins were playing to entertain guests prior to the evening ceremony.

"Well, I guess there's no backing out now," Roarke murmured to his older brother as they stood beneath the arbor of delicately fragrant wisteria and confederate jasmine.

Michael shot him a quick, warning look. "You're not thinking of taking off again?" Of all the brothers, Roarke seemed to have inherited the strongest strain of their father's wanderlust.

"Of course not," Roarke answered. "I told you, I've hung up my rambling shoes for good."

On cue, the toe-tapping strains of "The Lake Author Stomp" suddenly ceased. There was a strum of violin strings. And Roarke's face split into a wide grin as Daria Shea began walking up the aisle between the rows of folding chairs.

Her dark hair had been pinned up in some fancy style Michael suspected probably had a name and made her whiskey-hued eyes appear wider than usual. Her work as a prosecutor required her to dress in neat little tailored suits, which made the white lacy froth of a wedding dress—the kind a fairy-tale princess might have worn—even more surprising. Watching his brother's eyes darken with desire, Michael suspected that Roarke was not all that surprised by Daria's hidden romantic streak.

There was another strum of chords and Michael felt Shayne, standing on the other side of him, stand up straighter.

"Don't lock your knees," he advised beneath his breath. "Or you'll pass out."

"I think I just may anyway," Shayne admitted. "In fact, I'm afraid I'm having a heart attack."

"Join the club," Roarke said.

"Bliss is going to murder me if I die and leave her a widow before our wedding night."

"Geez," Michael muttered. "What's the matter with you two? After all you've both been through, this should be a piece of cake. It's only a wedding. What's the big deal?"

"Hey, don't get me wrong...I love the idea of being married," Shayne said. "It's all this pomp and ceremony that's so damn hard.... Damn, Bliss looks great though, doesn't she?"

"Gorgeous," Michael agreed.

It was true. Bliss Fortune's bright red curls were fired by the gold of the setting sun and her eyes were the same hue as the lacy Spanish moss an artistic florist had incorporated into her tiger lily bouquet. Diamonds that Michael knew had once belonged to her mother flashed at her earlobes. Her dress was a mere slip of ivory satin, cut high on the thigh. If Shayne hadn't already told him Bliss was carrying his child, Michael never would have known his landlady and about to be sister-in-law was pregnant.

He watched as she paused to hand her bouquet to her grandmother Zelda, who was sitting in the front row, beaming her pleasure beneath a wide-brimmed straw hat covered with blazing poppies.

Sitting next to Zelda were Mary and Patrick O'Malley. They were holding hands like young lovers and there'd been more than one time today Michael had witnessed their eyes meet in a way that hinted their reunion had been a success. Although he still couldn't understand how a man could take off for years, ostensibly deserting a woman he claimed to love, Michael was too happy to harbor a grudge toward his father. Especially since it seemed as if he really was home for good.

And there was no doubting the fact that Michael's mother hadn't stopped smiling since her errant husband's return. In fact, she was so happy Michael hadn't seen any point in bringing up those long-ago letters. Everything had worked out in the end, which was, he reminded himself, the important thing.

As Bliss took Shayne's hand, Michael's gaze drifted from his parents to Lorelei's. The Longstreets' behavior had undergone a change since that fateful day at the plantation house. When he and Lorelei had returned to town, Maureen, embracing him as if he'd been her own long-lost son, had tearfully proclaimed him a hero. And the good doctor, although not as effusive, had professed his own gratitude for Michael having rescued "his little girl."

Michael was relieved that the Longstreets had accepted him, after all these years. But the truth was, he could have lived with their antipathy, so long as Lorelei continued to love him. That was all that mattered.

There was a third strum of strings. And suddenly, Michael understood all too well what Roarke and Shayne were experiencing. His heart pounded painfully as Lorelei suddenly appeared, dressed in a deceptively simple calf-length white dress—cut on the bias, she'd told him, not that he'd understood the fashion term—that slid over her curves like a silk waterfall and brought to mind an ultraglamorous movie star from the forties.

She'd left her pale hair loose, as she knew he liked it, and forgoing a veil, had opted instead for a single white magnolia blossom pinned just above her ear.

"Close your mouth, big brother," Shayne murmured, his voice thick with humor. "You're going to catch fireflies."

Michael slammed his jaws shut. But he continued to stare at the ethereal vision that seemed to be floating toward him.

Her eyes, shimmering with heartfelt emotion, didn't move from his as she approached. Although her expression remained appropriately solemn, her lips were faintly curved in a private, secretive smile.

Although he'd never considered himself an even remotely romantic man, Michael knew he'd remember this day for the rest of his life. He was vaguely aware of his mother's quiet weeping, of the priest's calm voice, of his brothers repeating ancient vows.

As he heard Lorelei's clear voice ringing out like a silver bell, saying words spoken countless times by countless couples over the centuries, Michael felt as if he were hearing them for the very first time.

He took her smooth hand in his and slipped the wide gold band on her finger, pledging to love, honor and cherish her, for all time. Never had he taken a promise so seriously.

Lorelei viewed the unwavering resolve in his midnight eyes as he repeated the solemn vows and knew that to Michael, they were much more than mere ceremonial words. He'd always been the most responsible, dependable man she'd ever known. And now, wondrously, he was hers.

Her mind drifted momentarily as she wondered idly whether she should add a final scene to her script that Eric had assured her was the first of many he planned to produce and direct with her. At first she'd feared a wedding scene might be unnecessarily mushy.

But now, as she basked in the warmth of her husband's gaze and listened to the priest proclaim them man and wife, she decided that a romance was, by definition, mushy. So why should she deny her fictional heroine the ecstasy she was feeling?

"You may kiss your brides," the priest announced.

"It's about time," Roarke muttered.

"Finally," Shayne said at the same time. Both brothers had been forced to wait until Michael and Lorelei had repeated their vows.

As Michael touched his lips to Lorelei's, warmth flowed through her, a warmth as timeless and unending as the ancient land surrounding them. Laughing with pleasure, she flung her arms around his neck and kissed him back.

"Hey," Roarke interrupted after the kiss had gone on and on, "how about giving the rest of us a chance to kiss Hollywood's newest screenwriter?"

There was a bit of maneuvering as all three O'Malley brides were thoroughly kissed by all the brothers to the delight of gathered guests.

Then, as a heron took to the sky nearby with a flurry of blue wings, the band broke into a juiced-up Cajun rendition of the familiar wedding recessional.

With joy singing in her veins, Lorelei put her hand in Michael's. And together they walked back down the aisle into the blaze of a setting southern sun, toward their future.

# Take 4 bestselling love stories FREE

## Plus get a FREE surprise gift!

# DELTA JUSTICE

**A family dynasty of law and order
is shattered by a mysterious crime
of passion.**

Don't miss the second Delta Justice book
as the mystery unfolds in:

## *Letters, Lies and Alibis*
### by Sandy Steen

Rancher Travis Hardin is determined to right a
sixty-year wrong and wreak vengeance on the Delacroix.
But he hadn't intended to fall in love doing it. Was his
desire for Shelby greater than his need to destroy her
family?

Lawyer Shelby Delacroix never does anything halfway.
She is passionate about life, her work...and Travis. Lost
in a romantic haze, Shelby encourages him to join her in
unearthing the Delacroix family secrets. Little does she
suspect that Travis is keeping a few secrets of his own....

**Available in October
wherever Harlequin books are sold.**

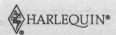

# HARLEQUIN WOMEN KNOW ROMANCE WHEN THEY SEE IT.

And they'll see it on **ROMANCE CLASSICS**, the new 24-hour TV channel devoted to romantic movies and original programs like the special **Romantically Speaking—Harlequin™ Goes Prime Time.**

**Romantically Speaking—Harlequin™ Goes Prime Time** introduces you to many of your favorite romance authors in a program developed exclusively for Harlequin® readers.

Watch for **Romantically Speaking—Harlequin™ Goes Prime Time** beginning in the summer of 1997.

*If you're not receiving ROMANCE CLASSICS, call your local cable operator or satellite provider and ask for it today!*

*Escape to the network of your dreams.*

See Ingrid Bergman and Gregory Peck in *Spellbound* on Romance Classics.

# Free Gift Offer

With a Free Gift proof-of-purchase
from any Harlequin® book, you can receive
a beautiful cubic zirconia pendant.

This stunning marquise-shaped stone is a genuine cubic
zirconia—accented by an 18" gold tone necklace.
(Approximate retail value $19.95)

## Send for yours today...
## compliments of ◈ HARLEQUIN®

To receive your free gift, a cubic zirconia pendant, send us one original proof-of-purchase, photocopies not accepted, from the back of any Harlequin Romance®, Harlequin Presents®, Harlequin Temptation®, Harlequin Superromance®, Harlequin Intrigue®, Harlequin American Romance®, or Harlequin Historicals® title available at your favorite retail outlet, together with the Free Gift Certificate, plus a check or money order for $1.65 U.S./$2.15 CAN. (do not send cash) to cover postage and handling, payable to Harlequin Free Gift Offer. We will send you the specified gift. Allow 6 to 8 weeks for delivery. Offer good until December 31, 1997, or while quantities last. Offer valid in the U.S. and Canada only.

# Free Gift Certificate

Name: _____

Address: _____

City: _____ State/Province: _____ Zip/Postal Code: _____

Mail this certificate, one proof-of-purchase and a check or money order for postage and handling to: HARLEQUIN FREE GIFT OFFER 1997. In the U.S.: 3010 Walden Avenue, P.O. Box 9071, Buffalo NY 14269-9057. In Canada: P.O. Box 604, Fort Erie, Ontario L2Z 5X3.

---

## FREE GIFT OFFER                                    084-KEZ

ONE PROOF-OF-PURCHASE
To collect your fabulous FREE GIFT, a cubic zirconia pendant, you must include this
original proof-of-purchase for each gift with the properly completed Free Gift Certificate.

---

084-KEZR